First published in Great Britain by Scribo MMXVII
Scribo, a division of Book House, an imprint of
The Salariya Book Company
25 Marlborough Place, Brighton, BN1 1UB
www.salariya.com

ISBN 978-1-912006-95-3

The right of Alex Woolf to be identified as the author of this work has been asserted
in accordance with sections 77 and 78 of the Copyright, Designs
and Patents Act, 1988.

Book Design by David Salariya

Condition of Sale

Printed and bound in China

The text for this book is set in Cochin
The display type is P22 Operina

www.salariya.com

Artwork Credits
Front cover illustration: John James
Gatefold illustrations: © Peter Jackson Collection / Look and Learn
Additional illustrations: John James

The Shakespeare Plot
Book 2

The Dark Forest

Alex Woolf

SCRIBO
a SALARIYA *imprint*

Act
One

Chapter 1

The Rescue

THE FOREST OF ARDEN, 24TH MARCH 1603

The young man moved silently through the forest. His feet padded softly upon the earth, negotiating the knotty roots of the ancient oak trees with the stealth of a wolf. An arrow lay against the notch of his handmade bow, ready to be fired. His hopeful, fearful eyes were ever on the alert for movement – be it caused by predator or prey. His clothes were no more than rags, his skin rough and dark.

Yesterday he had spent in similar fashion, and also the day before that. This was his life – forever on the move, never sleeping in the same place for more than one night. His only possessions were his bow and arrow, and his knife. Once, he supposed, he may have had a patch of earth where he belonged, somewhere he could call home. If so, he did not remember it. For countless moons, he had lived this way – a drifter, spurred onwards by the hope of finding food and by the fear of being found by the Evil One who was never far behind.

He was lonely, though he did not know it – for all he had ever been, at least in his memory, was alone. What most would call loneliness, he only felt as a melancholy emptiness at his core, a sense that there must be more to life than this endless cycle of hunger, thirst, fear and exhaustion.

In the afternoon, he chanced upon a babbling brook and he fell to the ground and drank greedily from it, not realising until that moment how parched he was. Shortly afterwards, he killed a squirrel for his evening meal, which he then tied by its tail to his belt. As the shafts of light through the forest canopy turned a reddish gold, he began to search for a place to rest his head for the night. As usual, he desired a spot easily camouflaged with branches and forest litter, but which also offered him a vantage point to watch for the Evil One. At length, he found a suitable spot beneath an enormous tree root growing out of the bank of a dried-up stream bed. He set about finding leafy branches to disguise and give added shelter to his new home. Once satisfied with his little den, the young man set about collecting firewood.

Dusk had fallen by the time he could rest his limbs by the crackling fire. He gutted the squirrel with his knife, skewered it with a sharpened stick, then began to turn it above the flames on a makeshift spit made from two forked branches. Even now, he did not relax his vigil on the trees, and his bow and arrow was always within easy reach.

As he lay upon his bed in the darkness, listening to the soft music of the crickets, frogs and night birds, he asked himself the same questions that tormented him every night. *Does the Evil One really exist? Why does it never show itself?* At times like these, the temptation arose simply to stay put – to make his latest shelter his home. But even in these moments he knew, in his heart, that he would never stop moving. For he was sure the Evil One *did* exist – whether it was truly evil or not the young man could not say – but it was always there. Sometimes, as he walked through the forest, he felt its presence close behind. Occasionally he might hear a rustle of leaves or the snap of a twig to his rear, but saw no animal nor any possible cause for the sound when he turned to look. Now and then he would hear a whisper, like the wind through branches, on a windless day. Once or twice he even fancied he felt the touch of a warm breath upon his neck.

At such times, he would always quicken his pace, and with nervous fingers he'd place an arrow at the ready in his bow – but he would not dare turn to see who or what was there.

The next morning, the young man rose before sunrise and destroyed his shelter and kicked over the ashes of his fire, removing all traces of his presence. With a fearful glance over his shoulder – for he sensed the Evil One close on his heels – he struck out into the forest, following an animal trail that he hoped might lead to a source of water and perhaps some breakfast.

The sun was about a quarter of the way through its arc and the young man was starting to feel the familiar pangs of hunger and thirst when he suddenly stopped and became extremely still. An unusual and frightening sound was coming through the trees from the north. It was the sound of human voices. The young man was not unacquainted with his own kind. From time to time, he had met and spoken to fellow wanderers in the forest. But those humans he had encountered had always been softly spoken – forest dwellers like himself. The voices he could hear now were sharp as thorns, and bitter as unripe berries. He sensed violence in their tone and it scared him. Keeping low to the ground, he crept closer to the source of the voices until he found himself on the edge of a clearing.

In its midst he spied three men on horseback. Two of them were threatening the third man with swords and pistols. The third man seemed angry rather than intimidated. He had a florid face, a full beard and long hair and was shouting at them to put down their weapons and let him pass. The men showed no signs of doing so. All he succeeded in doing was to make them angry, and soon enough one of them trotted up – a tall-looking fellow with a large, wide-brimmed hat – and struck the unarmed man hard on the side of the head with the flat of his sword. This caused him to topple off his horse and crash to the ground.

The young man, watching from behind a tree, flinched at the sight of this brutal act. He stared, appalled, as the two attackers dismounted and stood over the fallen figure, pointing their weapons at him. 'Hand over your money, wretch, and we might just let you live!' said the one in the hat.

The young man was, by nature, cautious, and his first instinct was to flee. And yet he felt sympathy for this brave man, and disgust at the savage treatment he was suffering at the hands of these bandits. He wanted to intervene, but remained hesitant. Why risk his own life by helping a stranger?

It was when the bandits began to kick their victim, hard, in the legs and torso, that the young man made up his mind. In one swift movement, he pulled an arrow from his quiver, drew his bow and fired. The arrow flew through the air and struck the shorter of the bandits in the leg. He screamed and fell over. The other bandit spun around to see where the arrow had come from. As he did so, another arrow shot out of the trees and pierced his hat. Then a third arrow whistled through the sleeve of his jerkin, narrowly missing his arm. This was all too much for the bandit. In two quick strides, he leapt onto his horse and galloped into the forest, leaving his wounded comrade still writhing around on the ground.

With the danger now gone, the young man emerged from his hiding-place. He ran to where the wounded bandit lay and removed the sword from his hand, in case he tried to attack him. Then he helped the other man to his feet.

'God grant you mercy, kind sir!' the man said hoarsely. 'That was quite exceptional shooting. I owe you my life.'

Unused to speech and somewhat embarrassed by this display of gratitude, the young man merely nodded.

'Is there anything I can do to repay you?'

The young man pointed to the water bottle attached to the saddle of the other man's horse.

'Why of course! Please drink!'

He handed him the bottle. After taking a deep and much needed draught, the young man handed it back, then turned and began to walk away.

'Prithee, do not go so soon,' said the man. 'Tell me who you are, at least, and how you come to be in these parts. Or am I to think you some guardian spirit of the forest sent here to protect unwary travellers? Tell me, are you flesh and blood?'

The young man paused in his stride and frowned at

this strange question.

'Whatever you are,' the man continued, 'I would welcome your companionship, not to mention your protection, for the remainder of my journey. I live not far from here, at a place called Bradenstoke Hall... But where are my manners? I should have introduced myself.' He gave a bow. 'I am Sir Griffin Markham, a soldier. And to whom do I owe the pleasure…?'

The young man did not reply. He was thinking: *What should I do? Should I go with him? I know nothing of this fellow. He may imprison or enslave me. On the other hand, he seems a kindly enough soul. Perhaps he will offer me food and shelter at this Bradenstoke Hall – and protection from the Evil One.*

He was interrupted in these thoughts by a groan from the wounded bandit. Glancing down, he saw the man had managed to pull the arrow from his leg, and had then fainted from the pain. The arrow head was slick with dark blood. The wound, however, was not too deep. It would heal if cared for.

Eventually, the young man came to a decision. He looked again at Sir Griffin Markham. 'I will go with you…' he said. The words sounded strange in his ears. His tongue felt thick and clumsy. It had been so long since he'd spoken.

Markham clapped his hands in delight. 'You speak! How splendid! And of your decision, I heartily approve!'

'We must take this one, too,' said the young man. 'He will die if we leave him here.'

'A fitting end for a no-good footpad such as he, wouldn't you say?' responded Markham as he remounted his horse. 'Come, let's leave him for the wolves. You can take his horse.'

The young man did not move, and Markham was forced to relent. 'Very well,' he sighed. 'We'll take him with us. There is a physician in the village who can tend to his leg.'

After heaving the unconscious bandit onto the back of his horse, the young man climbed into the saddle. He had no memory of riding, yet he found that his hands and legs knew what to do. Soon, he and Markham were riding side by side along the forest trail.

'You don't speak much,' commented Markham as they rode.

The young man glanced to the rear.

'And why do you keep doing that?' said Markham. 'You keep looking behind you. Are you being followed?'

Impatient at his companion's continued silence, Markham said at last: 'I must confess to an uncommon curiosity about you, young stranger. Pray tell me your story. From where do you hail?'

'I know not,' answered the young man truthfully. 'For as long as I can remember, I have been roaming these woods.'

'That is quite extraordinary!' declared Markham. 'Perhaps then I was right after all to call you a spirit of the forest. Do you recall nothing at all of your early life?'

After a pause the young man said: 'I remember once I had a name, though it is of little use to me now.'

'I wouldn't be so sure. For it will give me something by which to address you. What is it then – your name?'

'People used to call me… Richard Fletcher.'

Chapter 2

Sad Tidings

SOUTHWARK, 24TH MARCH 1603

Alice Fletcher stood at the corner of the stage at the Globe playhouse. She was watching the rehearsals of Shakespeare's play, *Twelfth Night*. It was a scene featuring a character called Sebastian. As always, she was reminded painfully of her long-lost brother Richard.

The play was about a pair of twins, Viola and Sebastian, who were separated in a shipwreck. Both were convinced that the other had drowned. In this scene, Sebastian was speaking of his grief to his friend Antonio: *She is drowned already, sir, with salt water, though I seem to drown her remembrance again with more.*

Alice, of course, identified with Sebastian's sister, Viola, especially so because the girl spent most of the play disguised as a boy – something Alice was obliged to do in her life as a player with the Chamberlain's Men. Just as Viola was forced to become Cesario, Alice had been obliged to reinvent herself as 'Adam'. The play was full of funny and romantic misunderstandings, with Viola falling in love with a man, who was in love with a woman, who was in love with Viola, thinking she was a man. But the part that always got to Alice like a stab in the heart was the ending, when the twins were reunited. It always made her cry. Of course, she had long ago given up hope of any such happy ending for herself.

The play was first performed on Candlemas night, 2 February 1602, almost exactly a year after Richard's disappearance – which made it all so much sadder for her. Gus Phillips, the unofficial leader of the Chamberlain's Men, had seemed to take a malicious pleasure in casting Alice as Viola. Gus was the only one in the company who knew Alice's secret, and clearly he found it hilarious to have a girl pretending to be a boy playing a girl pretending to be a boy. Alice had resisted at first, but was eventually persuaded when Shakespeare himself told her she should do it. In a strange way, she found that the role helped her with her grieving. It also went down very well with the audience, turning out to be one of the company's most popular productions of last year – so popular, they were now reviving it.

'You were born to play Viola.'

Alice jumped in surprise at the voice, so close to her ear. She turned to see Will Shakespeare standing by her side. He had the disconcerting habit of materialising like this sometimes. More disconcerting still was what he'd just said.

'*I?*' she said in confusion. 'Why do you say that, Mr Shakespeare?'

Had he guessed her secret? She often suspected that he had, but – unlike Gus – was too discreet to mention it.

'Your life experiences suit you to the role,' he replied enigmatically.

'You mean that I have lost my brother?'

He shrugged. 'Aye, that. But something else as well. You have always been an outsider here, Adam, much like Viola cast ashore in Illyria. Oh I know all of us players are misfits in one way or another. But you seem to be especially so. You have a haunted air, as if burdened by an inexpressible secret. I saw it first when you played Ophelia. And, it scarcely needs saying, you are highly adept at playing young women.'

Alice dared not reply, in case her voice betrayed her discomfort. Will was, whether he realised it or not, straying into dangerous waters.

He continued: 'Indeed, it was I who first mentioned to Gus that you should play the part.'

'I thought it was Gus's idea.'

'Of course!' smiled Will. 'All the best ideas are Gus's

– or so he wishes everyone to believe.'

'I find it hard… to play the final scene,' Alice confessed.

'The tears you shed are real then?'

'Aye. Though I'm looking at Mr Condell playing Sebastian, in my mind I always see Richard.'

'Do you still hope for his return?'

She shook her head. 'I long ago stopped hoping that my brother will come back. I accept that he's dead, but I will never stop mourning his loss.'

Alice glanced at Will Shakespeare. He had the demeanour of a contented, slightly plump gentleman of middle years – until one noticed his eyes. They were bright and alive as they met her gaze. Sometimes she wondered why he had chosen a lowly prentice like herself for a friend. Was he interested in her as a person, or as a basis for one of his characters? (Could she have even been an inspiration for Viola, for example?) Then she would chide herself for such unworthy thoughts. She should be grateful that such a celebrated man would consider her a friend. Although, if truth be told, it was an odd, one-sided sort of friendship, for they only ever seemed to talk about her. Will rarely spoke of himself. Perhaps it was time to change that.

'But you must know all about missing loved ones, Mr Shakespeare,' she said. 'You have a family in Stratford-upon-Avon whom you hardly ever see.'

His smile faded and his bearing became cooler, leaving Alice with the impression that she had trespassed on very private territory. 'I see my family when I can,' he said, and he moved away from her. She felt the sting of his displeasure. It angered her. What right did he have to be annoyed by an innocent observation?

'But it is never enough,' she heard him mutter, almost to himself. Alice glanced towards him. 'I missed seeing my daughters grow up,' he said. 'I was here, in London, when the plague took my only son in his twelfth year. I was here also when my father followed him to the grave a few years hence. My daughters barely know me. My wife is a mute and faded ghost of the woman I married. My mother is alone. My separation from them has been like a long winter. I have been productive – I have achieved wealth and renown – but such things can feel a little hollow when weighed against the cost to myself and those I love.'

He turned from her and continued on his way. Then he paused in his stride as Gus Phillips appeared at the entrance of the Tiring-House at the back of the stage. Gus's normally ruddy cheeks were pale. He looked shaken and distracted. 'I have just now been to the city,' he said, leaning against the door frame and mopping his brow. 'Alas, I have heard it announced on every street corner…'

The players had, by now, stopped their rehearsing, and were all staring as one at Gus.

'Heard what?' cried Henry Condell. 'Speak, Gus!'

'Sad tidings,' Gus sighed. 'The queen – God-a-mercy! – she's dead…'

There was a stunned silence as the players absorbed

this news. Who could imagine it? Elizabeth, queen of England for almost forty-five years, dead. No one present could remember a time before her reign.

'She passed away in the small hours of last night, peacefully in her bed,' said Gus.

'She was becoming frail,' said John Heminges. 'We should have expected this.'

'Yet none of us did,' said Robert Armin.

Alice remembered the proud, dignified, rather splendid lady she had met two years earlier on her visit to Whitehall Palace. Though old, she had appeared full of vigour, asking Alice questions and flirting with Burbage. It was hard to think of her now still and lifeless.

Gus then posed a question that most had not even got around to considering: 'I wonder who will succeed her – and what it will mean for us…?'

Chapter 3

A Flash Like No Other

LONDON, 28TH APRIL 1603

Tom Cavendish watched the thick, greenish liquid bubbling and smoking away in the crucible suspended over the furnace. It looked like something conjured from the pits of hell, he thought, as it threatened to rise up and spill over the sides of the vessel.

His master, Sir Francis Bacon, was watching it, too. 'Methinks it is ready,' said Sir Francis, and with a pair of iron tongs, he lifted the crucible from the fire and carefully poured the still-frothing liquid through a filter of old cloth into a cauldron.

They were in a gloomy chamber in the basement of York House, surrounded by a clutter of equipment used by Sir Francis for his experiments in alchemy. Glass and copper flasks lined the shelves, alongside odd-shaped retorts, alembics, funnels, tubes and vials. A huge book lay open on a table, next to a pestle and mortar for crushing things to powder.

'Boil up some water for me, Tom,' called Sir Francis as he dipped his quill in an inkwell and scribbled a few notes in the book.

Tom rushed to fill another cauldron from a bucket of water collected earlier from the well, then hooked it over the fire. Nothing was more pleasurable to him than these hours spent helping Sir Francis with his experiments. This man was, after all, one of the foremost natural philosophers in the land, pushing back the very frontiers of human knowledge. Tom could not believe his good fortune at being allowed to take part in the great man's investigations.

'I want to create the brightest flash ever seen,' Sir Francis had announced a few weeks earlier. 'We've all seen the modest sparkle of a playhouse firecracker. Well, I want something much more dazzling. I want it to rival a bolt of lightning, or a beam of sunlight as it strikes the eye. And what is the only way to achieve this, Tom?'

'By experiment, sir.'

'By experiment, indeed. And what substances do you propose that we use for our experiment?'

'Um, sulphur and… aluminium powder, sir.'

'I've taught you well, Tom. Aye, we'll need both of those. But you have left out one other important ingredient: chlorate of potash.'

'Chlorite of potash…?'

'Indeed. Well, nearly…'

'Would you like me to purchase some from the apothecary, sir?'

'No, Tom. The chlorate of potash sold by apothecaries is a very inferior product. We shall need to create our own. By a process of trial and error, we shall endeavour to produce an extremely pure form of this substance, and mix it in the correct proportion with the sulphur and the aluminium powder.'

Every day since then they had brewed up new batches of the formula, each time making small adjustments to the recipe – adjustments that Sir Francis would carefully record in his big book. Along the way, they had achieved some spectacular flashes, some of which had been so bright they had left both of them partially blind for minutes on end.

But Sir Francis was never satisfied. 'Not bright enough,' he would mutter. 'We must try again.'

Today was their fifteenth attempt at this experiment, and Tom was hopeful they were getting close. After several more rounds of boiling, filtering, dissolving and then re-boiling the mixture, they were left with a pile of greenish white crystals nestling at the bottom of the crucible. Sir Francis picked out one of these and held it up to the firelight. He sniffed it, then poked out the tip of his tongue and licked it. Finally, in solemn tones, he declared: 'I do believe that this may be the purest batch of chlorate of potash ever created on this Earth.'

'Truly, sir?' said Tom, staring at the crystals in wonder.

Sir Francis nodded. 'Hurry now Tom, fetch the sulphur and the aluminium powder.'

Previous experiments had revealed the most effective proportions of the three substances to be four measures of chlorate to two of sulphur and two of aluminium. Using a spoon, Tom carefully scooped out the correct amounts of yellow sulphur and silver-grey aluminium powder. Sir Francis watched tensely as he mixed them together with the chlorate crystals.

'That's enough,' said Sir Francis after a few minutes. He lit a taper in the fire and held the flame above the mixture. 'Hide your eyes if you wish, Tom.'

He said this every time, and every time Tom replied: 'I prefer to watch, sir. That way we can both bear witness.'

'Are you sure? This time will be very bright.'

'I'm sure, sir.'

Sir Francis lowered the taper and the flame touched the mixture.

The flash seemed impossibly bright – almost blue in its whiteness – and it illuminated the gloomy basement room as if the entire building above them had suddenly and miraculously disappeared, exposing all to sunlight. It seared Tom's eyes, forcing them closed. When it faded just a second or so later, the burning brightness persisted in his retinas so that he could see only that and nothing else.

'I am blind, sir,' he said.

'I, too,' confessed Sir Francis.

'Verily, that was a flash like no other. People will say you have stolen lightning from the very heavens.'

Sir Francis chuckled. 'They may well be right.'

Tom strained his eyes, but could see nothing beyond a bleached white desert. He heard Sir Francis stumble towards the table so that he could record the success in his book.

'Zounds!' cursed the philosopher. 'I've spilled the ink.'

They both heard the scrape of a footstep on the stairway descending from the upper floor.

'Who goes there?' cried Sir Francis.

'It's only me, sir,' said a voice from above.

Sir Francis sighed. 'And who, pray, is me?'

'Why, don't you know me, sir? Tis Owen, the groom.'

Owen Jennings had been, like Tom, a servant at Essex House, and Tom had persuaded Sir Francis to offer him employment at York House following the Earl of Essex's downfall.

'Ah, Owen,' exclaimed Sir Francis. 'I do apologise, my eyes are temporarily indisposed.'

They heard Owen walk down a few more steps. 'Have you and Tom been playing with that flash powder again, sir?' asked the groom. 'I fear you may soon land yourselves in trouble with the law, just like my previous master – that is, if you don't kill yourselves first. I'm sure the new king will not be pleased to hear about people setting off gunpowder in basements...'

'This is not gunpowder, Owen,' said Sir Francis. 'And our purpose is not violence against the king or anyone else, but the pursuit of knowledge. Where there was darkness, we are bringing light.'

'A little too much light in this case, perhaps,' muttered Tom, his eyes still in shock.

'What is it you want, Owen?' asked Sir Francis.

'Sire, tis the day of the royal funeral, and you are one of the official mourners. You are expected at the Palace where the queen's body is waiting for you to escort it to Westminster Abbey.'

'By Minerva, you are right!' cried Sir Francis. 'The queen cannot be kept waiting on this of all days. Prithee, Tom, guide me to my carriage, for I cannot see a thing.'

'Neither can I, sir.'

With Owen's help, Sir Francis and Tom were guided to the carriage and conveyed to Whitehall Palace. During the journey there, the white cloud in which Tom had dwelt since the flash gradually became a misty veil through which he could begin to make out the outlines of the world. He was not allowed to accompany the coffin, so he took up position on Parliament Street, along with thousands of other Londoners come to pay their last respects to the queen. Others gathered at upper-storey windows and even perched on rooftops to watch the funeral cortège pass by.

Elizabeth's coffin, covered in purple velvet, was drawn by four horses draped in black livery. Atop the coffin lay a life-size sculpture of the queen wearing her crown and robes of state and carrying a sceptre. Six knights walked alongside the coffin, sheltering it with a canopy. As the cortège swayed through the streets, the crowd gasped at the sight of the lifelike sculpture on the coffin, and many began to weep. Following along behind the hearse were more than a thousand official mourners, all dressed in black. Among them was Sir Francis Bacon, still barely able to see. At one point he accidentally veered away from the pack and began wandering up a side street until he was dragged back into line by the Marquis of Northampton.

One notable absentee from the funeral was the queen's successor, King James I. He was the son of Elizabeth's cousin, Mary Queen of Scots, and already the ruler of Scotland (where he was known as James VI). Although he left Edinburgh on 5 April, his progress southwards was slow, with frequent stops to enjoy the hospitality of local lords, and he was not due to arrive in London until the end of May.

Tom watched the funeral procession go by and he wept along with everyone else – though his tears were not prompted by sadness, but were merely a delayed reaction to the flash. In truth, he had never felt any great affection for a monarch who had behaved so cruelly to his former master, Essex. Of course, Essex was a vain and foolish man – he had learned that much – but knowing this did not alter his impression of the queen as a callous, unfeeling woman. If only she could have been more understanding of Essex, her former favourite, Tom was sure he would never have been tempted to rebel against her.

'Tom Cavendish?'

The voice drifted out from the crowd behind him. He would know those soft, husky tones anywhere. He whirled around. 'Alice?'

Through the veil of his defective vision there swam a sea of ghostly faces. He turned this way and that, seeking her out. Finally, he spotted her, shimmering in a halo of blurry light, and he started towards her. But when he took hold of her arm, she brushed him away. 'Unhand me, knave!' she said, now sounding very much like an old lady.

What was going on? Had he imagined it?

'Are you blind, Tom?' came Alice's voice again. 'Here I am.'

This time, he felt her hand on *his* arm.

'Alice?'

'Adam!' she corrected him. 'Remember?'

'Forgive me!'

He could make out the vague shape of her smile, and his heart beat faster. It was always such a pleasure to see her.

'Why are you blind today?' she asked.

Tom wiped his eyes. 'Sir Francis went a little far with

one of his experiments,' he said. 'Look!' He put a hand in his pocket and pulled out some of the alchemical mixture, which he had secreted there earlier. 'Set this alight and it will make a flash brighter than the sun.'

Alice took a small pinch of it from Tom's palm and rubbed it between her fingers. 'We could use this for our visual effects at the Globe,' she said, and sniffed it. 'Sulphur and... something else. What's in it?'

'That's a secret.'

'Your loyalty to your master is admirable, Tom,' she smirked, 'but do not doubt that I shall find out the recipe. Does it include chlorate of potash?'

Tom thought it wisest to change the subject. 'So how is life these days at the Globe?' he asked.

She grinned, accepting defeat – for now.

'It's interesting, you might say!' she said. 'We seesaw between misery and ecstasy with each passing week, as new announcements keep arriving from the king. Last week, we were told that he had banned Sunday plays – Sunday, of course, being the day we get our biggest audiences. The king did this, so we were informed, to 'protect the Sabbath' – in other words, to keep his new friends the Puritans happy. So the people will go and play football instead and the churches will remain just as empty, while we poor players starve. And then, just as we were all about to throw ourselves into the Thames in despair, there came some astonishingly good news: King James wishes to be patron of our company! Would you believe it, Tom? Henceforth, you are to refer to us as the King's Men.' She laughed. 'You should have seen Gus when he heard about it. He did this jig of crazed delight that nearly sent him crashing off the stage.'

'Well, congratulations!' said Tom. 'That should keep you all secure in your jobs for as long as James remains on the throne.'

'Or until we put on a play that he and his Puritan friends decide they don't like,' grimaced Alice. 'We live in very uncertain times.'

Tom nodded. 'To think, just a few weeks ago, the Catholics were so hopeful that James would grant them religious toleration. Now they're being persecuted again.'

The Catholics had had every reason to be hopeful. James, after all, was the son of the Catholic monarch Mary Queen of Scots. Even though he was brought up a Protestant, he was very welcoming to the English Catholics who visited him in Scotland after it was announced that he would be their next king. He called the Roman church the 'Mother church', and told them that Catholics who refused to attend Anglican services would no longer need to pay their fines.

'I wonder why he changed his mind about the fines,' wondered Alice.

'According to Sir Francis, it was because he took one look at the state of the royal treasury and saw how much he needed the money.'

'I feel sorry for the Catholics, having their hopes

dashed like that,' said Alice. 'James is being even harder on them than Elizabeth was. If they miss one payment of those fines, they can lose everything they own, even their homes – and all they want to do is follow their own religion. What's so bad about that?'

Tom had no answer to this question.

They returned their attention to the endless column of mourners slowly making their way towards the Abbey where the queen would be laid to rest. Beyond them, Tom noticed an even grimmer procession taking place in one of the back alleys that lay just off Parliament Street. A series of carts were clattering over the cobbles. Piled up inside them, he glimpsed the stiff, pale limbs of corpses, with swollen boils visible on their skin – plague victims. It was not uncommon on London's streets to see the odd dead body being carted away, but it was rare to see so many of them.

The plague seemed especially bad this year...

Act Two

Chapter 4

The Holy Struggle

BRADENSTOKE HALL, 1ST MAY 1603

Richard Fletcher held the bowstring taut as he squinted along the arrow shaft at the target. Head cocked to one side, knuckles pressed firmly against his cheek, legs slightly apart, his body was in perfect balance. He slowed his breathing until the arrow tip was completely steady, then released the string. The bow twanged and the arrow hissed through the air, striking the heart of the target.

The target was a man – or, rather, it was a piece of wood crudely carved into the shape of a man. It was positioned some thirty paces from where Richard was standing. The only puzzling thing about the wooden man was the thing it was wearing on its head. Richard had no idea why the woodcarver had given the figure a crown.

'Fine shooting, my friend,' said a nearby voice.

Richard turned. He was surprised to see Jake Heathcock standing there, leaning on a walking stick. Jake was the bandit he'd shot in the forest, and then taken back here. He'd been tended by the local physician, and was now living in a labourer's cottage in the village. His wounded leg was looking better.

'You're walking now,' Richard observed.

'Aye,' said Jake cheerfully. He squinted at the target, with the arrow stuck in the middle of its heart. 'Though I wouldn't have been if you'd hit me there. I'd have been dead, for sure.'

Richard nodded his head. He didn't know what to say, a common problem for him. Even now, more than a month since he arrived here, he found the art of human conversation extremely tricky.

'How are things with you?' asked Jake.

'Sir Griffin has been very kind,' Richard replied. 'I want for nothing.'

'You're happy then?'

'Aye – well, sort of.' He hadn't expected to confide in Jake, but the words slipped out almost accidentally. 'I haven't been sleeping too well lately, in fact. I've been afflicted by strange dreams.'

'Dreams?'

'Aye. I dreamt last night that I was standing on a

wooden stage, surrounded by hundreds of people, saying words – words I had learned, written by another man. And then… I forgot what I was supposed to say, and all these hundreds of people started laughing at me.'

It had been a horrible dream, and Richard shuddered to recall it. He also felt faintly embarrassed to have even mentioned it to Jake.

Luckily, Jake did not seem to have been listening very closely. 'I'm sorry to hear that,' he said in a distracted tone, his thoughts clearly elsewhere.

'Will you go back to being a bandit, now you're better?' Richard asked him.

'Not likely!' laughed Jake. 'There's plenty of honest work to be had hereabouts. Ploughing, sheep shearing, that sort of thing. My hope is I can save up enough to buy myself a pig.'

'I wish you well with that.'

'I wanted to thank you, Richard, for bringing me back here,' said Jake, his smile fading. 'I know it was you who insisted. Sir Griffin, for sure, would have been happy to leave me to die in that forest, after what I did.'

Again, Richard was stuck for words.

'I wanted to… return the favour,' added Jake in a hesitant tone, 'and warn you about something…'

Richard looked up, curious.

'This place,' said Jake, '– these people – here at Bradenstoke Hall. They're not quite what they seem…'

'What do you mean?'

'I mean there may be danger… you may be in danger.'

'What sort of danger would that be, Goodman Heathcock?' asked a deep voice behind them.

Jake spun around, and nearly keeled over when he saw who it was. Struggling to regain his balance with his stick, he stammered: 'N-Nothing, Sir Griffin. I m-misspoke, sir.'

Sir Griffin Markham fixed him with a puzzled frown. 'If there's something on your mind, sirrah, I want to hear it.'

'I m-must go, sir,' said Jake, hobbling away as fast as he could. 'Promised Old Henry Bishop I'd mend his plough.'

Markham and Richard watched him go. 'Strange fellow,' muttered Markham. 'I wonder what he meant.' Then he spotted the arrow in the wooden man, and his face broke into a smile. 'Did you put that in there from here?'

Richard nodded.

'That's very impressive, young man! You know, we could use a talented archer like you.'

'Use me for what?'

'For the struggle.'

Richard looked at him blankly.

'I mean the struggle for survival,' explained Markham. 'We Catholics, don't you know, are engaged in a war against those who would destroy us. We need soldiers, fighting men…'

'Catholics,' muttered Richard. The word troubled

him. His mind flickered with images of an invading armada, of people meeting in darkened rooms clutching rosaries and muttering prayers in Latin, and a dead priest hanging from a gallows.

'Aye,' said Markham. 'I am a Catholic – one of those who stayed true to the old faith. That's why I don't go to the church in the village on Sundays. I prefer to pay the fine and keep my soul pure. When I can, I attend mass in secret, although it's getting harder, with most of England's priests gone to ground or killed.' He glanced at Richard. 'I haven't told you this before, but I hope I can trust you. I know you won't speak of it to anyone.' Markham chuckled to himself. 'You remember that day last month, just after you came here, when a message arrived from London and I laughed and danced around the room.'

'I remember,' said Richard, his face creasing into a smile. How could he forget? He'd actually believed his host had lost his wits. 'You laughed because… because Queen Elizabeth was dead.'

Markham nodded. 'Indeed I did! And can you blame me? She more than anyone was responsible for the campaign to wipe us out. I was so happy when she died and James became king. James, son of Mary, the Catholic queen of Scots. And he seemed at first to prove himself his mother's boy by making us a solemn vow to cease the persecution, abolish the fines, and allow us to practise our religion in peace. We began to dream that the dark times were over… How wrong we were!

Just two weeks later came a royal pronouncement: there would be no change to Elizabeth's anti-Catholic laws. Indeed, the fines would be increased.'

Markham ground his teeth and gazed bitterly into the distance. 'That was a black day – the day when the flame of all my hopes turned to ash and cinders. That was the day when I knew there would be no end to our torment, not in any future I could foresee – for who could say how long his reign would last.'

He paused, glancing at Richard for signs of a response. 'What would *you* do in such circumstances, young man? Roll over? Accept that you're doomed? Or take up arms and fight?'

Richard was, as usual, lost for words.

'Will you join us?' Markham asked him. 'As I said, we could use a man of your talents.'

Luckily, Markham didn't push Richard for an answer. He wondered what exactly Markham wanted him to do, and his eyes fell once again upon the wooden man with the arrow in his heart and the crown upon his head.

Later that afternoon, Richard walked into the village to seek out Jake Heathcock. He wanted to ask him what he'd meant when he said Richard may be in danger. But Jake was not at home, nor at Old Henry Bishop's farm, nor at the inn. No one had seen him anywhere, in fact. So Richard returned, dissatisfied and slightly uneasy in his thoughts, to Bradenstoke Hall.

As he approached the house, he was struck for the first time how like a traditional castle it was. The building was surrounded by a large, rectangular moat, accessed by a footbridge. The gatehouse, with its narrow, arrowslit windows, was topped by battlements where archers could conceal themselves. Bradenstoke Hall seemed to crouch defensively like a fox, rather than standing proud like a stag. It almost seemed to expect attack.

That evening, Richard joined Sir Griffin Markham in the great hall for a meal of wild boar followed by honey and cinnamon tart. Markham asked Richard where he'd gone to that afternoon, and for the first time Richard found himself lying to his host.

'I went hunting in the forest,' he said.

'Ah, did you catch anything?'

'Nothing bigger than a hare,' he muttered.

Markham smiled, and for a long time he was silent, focusing instead on the meat on his plate and the ale in his tankard.

'We English Catholics,' he said eventually, 'are like the harts and hares of the forest – hunted and butchered simply because of what we are. For nigh on seventy years we have been treated as strangers in our own land; our priests and those who harbour them have been tortured and killed in their hundreds. They have been subjected to the rack, which stretches their bodies past breaking point, and to the 'scavenger's daughter', a terrible device that compresses them enough to force blood from their nose and ears. They have been hanged and then, while still alive, cut down, disembowelled and beheaded. Yet never did I hear of any priest, even in the midst of such torments, renounce their faith.'

Richard listened to all this with a dry mouth, his appetite quite gone. He watched as Markham rose to his feet and moved over to the hearth. From a shelf above it, he took down a richly jewelled, glass-fronted vessel, and carried it to where Richard sat.

'See this,' he said in hushed tones, pointing to a small and slender bone lying on a velvet cushion inside the vessel. 'This is from the hand of James Bodey, a priest of York, martyred in 1582. While he was hanging from the gallows, choking to death on the rope, Bodey raised that same hand to heaven and made the sign of the cross. He forgave his executioners even as they cut him down and performed their unspeakable rituals upon his dying person. His severed head was placed upon a spike on one of the city gates of York. It was later rescued by his flock, and embalmed as a relic. Indeed, within a day of his death, every single part of his body had been carried away by the faithful. I was fortunate enough to obtain this finger bone as a young man, and whenever I ride into battle, I wear it on a chain around my neck beside my crucifix.'

Markham placed the reliquary upon the table next to Richard's plate, so the blessed finger seemed to point directly at him.

'Join us,' urged Markham. 'Help us in our holy struggle to restore England to the True Faith.'

With an effort, Richard tore his gaze from Bodey's finger. He glanced up, only to find Markham standing over him, very close. He was watching Richard expectantly, with a feverish kind of light in his eyes. Richard could not remember being subjected to such intense scrutiny. His kindly, amiable host was behaving most oddly tonight. Of course, Richard could not fail to be moved by Markham's account of the persecution of English Catholics. He felt very sad for all they had suffered. Yet he also knew for certain he was not one of them. This was not his fight.

He wondered how to say this tactfully to a man who had given him so much. Would Markham even accept no for an answer? In some ways, he wished he had never accepted Markham's offer of hospitality. Even though his life in the forest had been tough, having to cope with the presence of the Evil One and the constant pangs of hunger, at least he had been free and not beholden to anyone but himself.

'I–,' he began.

'You'll do it!' said Markham excitedly, mistaking the word for *Aye*.

'Nay,' said Richard. 'What I mean to say is, I cannot join you. Pray forgive me. You have been very kind, Sir Griffin. But this is *your* struggle, not mine. If you want to send me away, I will understand.'

Markham's smile died. He breathed out slowly, and

his face turned sad, as if he was exhaling joy as well as air.

'Of course I won't send you away,' he said somewhat stiffly. 'You are my guest, Richard, and you shall remain at Bradenstoke Hall.'

Richard smiled appreciatively, even though he was a little troubled by Markham's tone, which sounded a lot more like a command than an invitation.

There came a loud clatter of hoofbeats on the courtyard cobblestones outside. A moment later, the door of the great hall burst open and in strode a tall, impressive-looking man. He had dark, angry-looking eyes and a small black pointed beard. His towering, wide-brimmed black hat added yet more inches to his height.

'Greetings, Catesby!' said Markham. 'How do you fare?'

'As well as can be expected in these bleak times,' the man replied dourly, handing his hat and cloak to Hastings, the groom, who had followed him in. Catesby wore an olive-green doublet with padded shoulders, which emphasized his muscular build.

'May I introduce my guest, Richard Fletcher,' said Markham. 'Richard, this is Robert Catesby, an old friend and fellow Catholic.'

'Well met,' muttered Catesby before turning to Markham. 'Got any sack, my friend? I am in need of refreshment after my journey from London.'

Richard stole another glance at Catesby as Hastings poured him a goblet of fortified wine. There was something familiar about the man. He was sure he'd seen him before – perhaps in his life before the forest…

'How goes it in the capital?' asked Markham.

'All is proceeding as planned,' replied Catesby. 'A certain lady will be arriving here later this evening.'

'We are ready to receive her,' said Markham.

A certain lady…? Richard wondered who they could be talking about.

Markham spotted Richard's bewilderment and laughed. 'Have no fear, young Richard. I will tell you everything – once you have sworn loyalty to our cause.'

Catesby's face darkened on hearing this. 'You mean he isn't one of us?'

'He will be,' smiled Markham. 'He just needs a little more time to come round to the idea.'

The visitor looked far from reassured. In fact, he was furious. 'Why is he even here, in this room, in that case? He should not be privy to our discourse. This is all far too risky.' Catesby then turned on Richard, causing him to flinch. 'And why, by all the saints, do you need more time, sirrah? You know our plight! Is it not yet clear to you where your allegiance should lie?'

'Let him alone, Catesby!' said Markham, drawing him away from Richard. 'You are always so on edge. Remember, during the Essex Rebellion two years ago, you were just the same…'

'Aye, and was I not right to be worried?' spat Catesby. 'We should have known better than to throw our hats in with that Protestant popinjay.'

'If he had succeeded, a Catholic might have ended up on the throne.'

'If he had succeeded!' Catesby scowled. 'The man was a fool-born, craven-hearted coxcomb, and most of you were too blind to see it. You may have got off lightly, Markham, but I was captured, remember, and fined 4,000 marks, forcing me to sell my estate at Chastleton.' He sighed, and cast another menacing glance towards Richard. 'But we won't make that mistake again.'

'Indeed not,' said Markham heartily. 'This time, nothing will go wrong.'

'I'll drink to that,' said Catesby swigging down the rest of his sack and slamming the goblet on the table. 'I must away, Markham. This is the last leg of my journey.'

'Where are you staying?'

'With my cousin, Bess Throckmorton, at her family home at Coughton Court, ten miles from here.'

'Prithee, pass on my heartiest good wishes to Bess, and to Sir Walter.'

'I shall,' answered Catesby as he took his hat from Hastings and replaced it on his head.

It was then that Richard saw something that caused him to remember where he'd seen this man before. What he saw was an arrow hole right in the middle of Robert Catesby's hat.

Richard rose nervously to his feet, pushing back his chair. 'Wait!' he said.

Catesby, who had been on his way out of the room,

paused in mid-stride and turned, eyebrows raised in surprise. 'So your guest has a tongue, Markham?'

'Why are you here?' Richard asked. 'I don't understand.'

Catesby smiled. 'Why am I here, Markham?'

'For my sack, certainly,' replied Markham. 'For my company, perhaps a distant second.'

'I s-saw you, in the forest,' Richard almost shouted. 'You were robbing Sir Griffin.' He pointed a shaking finger at Catesby's headwear. 'I put that hole through your hat.'

Chapter 5

A Visit to the Clink

LONDON, 1ST MAY 1603

On the first morning of May 1603, disturbing news blew like a January wind through the corridors of Whitehall Palace: Lady Arbella Stuart, cousin of the king, had gone missing. Three days earlier, she had vanished from the garden of her home at Hardwick Hall in Derbyshire. Despite an extensive search of the grounds and the surrounding area, not a trace of her had been found, nor any clue to her disappearance.

This was especially worrying for the king's chief minister and spymaster Robert Cecil because he knew that Lady Arbella had long been a target of England's enemies. Rebel Catholics – or 'papists', as Cecil liked to call them – viewed Arbella as a potential heir to the throne, and someone they could manipulate if they could get hold of her.

During Elizabeth's reign there had been several plots by papists to replace the queen with Arbella. Although the noblewoman was herself Protestant, the conspirators believed she harboured Catholic sympathies. Their plan was to install her on the throne, then marry her to a European prince, who would restore England to the true faith. That this did not happen was thanks in large part to Cecil and his network of spies. The plots were foiled, Queen Elizabeth died peacefully in her bed and was succeeded by King James. Arbella, meanwhile, continued to lead her quiet life at Hardwick Hall.

Until now…

Tom had spent the morning helping Sir Francis with his magnetic experiments. Sir Francis had become terribly excited about magnets, ever since reading William Gilbert's book on the subject. Tom, of course, relished every minute spent with his master in his basement laboratory. So far they had discovered how to make ordinary metals magnetic by rubbing them with a magnet; how to increase a magnet's strength by striking it with a hammer; and how to reduce its strength by heating it. Sir Francis declared that his ultimate aim was to prove Gilbert's theory that the

Earth itself was a giant magnet. Unfortunately, Tom was unable to continue with his master on this thrilling quest, because just then an urgent message arrived summoning him to Whitehall Palace.

'You're wanted by the chief minister,' announced Sir Francis in grave tones.

'I, sir?' said Tom disbelievingly.

'Something urgent, apparently.'

'But, sir, we have so much more to learn about magnets…'

'No matter,' said Sir Francis breezily. 'The secrets of the universe can wait until another day. The king's business cannot.'

An hour later, Tom was ushered into Cecil's austere and gloomy office in Whitehall Palace. He was astonished – and extremely happy – to see Alice there, dressed as usual in her boy outfit. She was standing before the chief minister, who was seated at his desk.

Cecil – his dark attire matching the sombre colours of the room – was a famously short man, with a long face and beard. His sharp eyes seemed to notice everything – including the smile that Alice flashed at Tom as he came and stood beside her. Cecil's enemies called him the Beagle for his small stature, yet there was a grudging compliment in the nickname, too, for beagles are well known for their tenacity and skill as hunting dogs.

He came straight to the point. 'You two did sterling

service for this country during the Essex Rebellion two years ago. Now a new crisis has blown up and I need you once again. Are you willing to help me?'

'Sir Francis is in the middle of writing a book on his experimental methods, my lord, and he needs my assistance,' said Tom.

'The King's Men have never been so busy,' added Alice. 'I'm due to play Portia in *The Merchant of Venice* tomorrow afternoon…'

Cecil hushed them both with impatient flaps of his hands. 'This is far more important than any of that,' he said. 'Sir Francis and the King's Men will survive a day or two without you. Now, have either of you heard of Lady Arbella Stuart…?'

So that was that. Cecil had asked them if they were available, but wasn't really offering them a choice. They had been recruited for this task before they had even entered his office.

'Rebel Catholics have been plotting to install Arbella on the throne for years,' explained Cecil. 'And now I'm certain they've kidnapped her, which can mean only one thing: they're planning a coup. They're going to try and topple James and replace him with Arbella. The poor lady wants nothing to do with any of this, of course. All she's ever desired is a quiet life – but when you're the great-great-granddaughter of King Henry VII, and the papists are casting around for an alternative monarch – a quiet life is never going to be your destiny. Sad to say, she has become a pawn of this ruthless band, bent on overturning the rightful government of our realm and taking power, through her, for themselves.'

'And what can we do?' asked Alice. 'Would you like us to find her?'

Cecil shook his head. 'That would be next to impossible. She could be anywhere in the country by now, or even abroad. No, what I need from you two is some good old-fashioned spy work…'

Tom and Alice looked at each other, wondering what he could mean.

'There's a priest named William Watson, currently serving time in the Clink Prison,' explained Cecil. 'Watson has been involved in several previous plots to capture Lady Arbella. If anyone knows who the kidnappers are, it'll be him. The trouble is, he won't confess what he knows, not even under threat of torture. The man's as hard as nails. He also knows all my regular spies by sight... But he doesn't know you two. If you could meet with Watson, befriend him, you might just be able to obtain some information about the plot. Even the smallest clue would help.'

Tom emitted an audible gulp. He didn't relish visiting a squalid prison, nor did he much like the sound of William "hard as nails" Watson.

'When do you want us to go?' asked Alice.

'This afternoon,' said Cecil. 'My agent will provide you with suitable clothing and cover stories. The gaoler will be made aware of the plan, as will his guards. They will come to your aid should things get out of hand.'

'Are things likely to… get out of hand?' wondered Tom nervously.

'You never know,' said Cecil. 'Watson may be a man of the cloth, but he has a quite a vicious reputation. So long as he believes you're fellow prisoners, and Catholics, I'm sure he'll be charming. But if he suspects either of you are spies, well…' Cecil gave a pained smile. 'Let's just hope the guards are in time to rescue you…'

Some hours later, Alice and Tom were standing outside the big iron-studded door of the Clink Prison in Southwark. They were dressed in grubby old shirts and leggings with holes in them. From the other side of the door, they could hear Cecil's agent, Robert Poley, in muffled conversation with the gaoler. Alice and Tom had been told to wait outside until they were called for.

'I don't care for this plan one bit,' confessed Tom as he eyed the grim exterior of the prison with its high wall and iron-barred windows. 'It's not fair. We helped out Cecil once, and now it's as if he owns us. Why should we be forced to risk our lives whenever he snaps his fingers?'

'Don't fret, Tom,' said Alice. 'Remember how we broke into a heavily defended Essex House. This will be easy by comparison.'

Tom frowned, puzzled and slightly irritated by her attitude. 'Why are you so keen anyway? Don't tell me you're doing this for king and country.'

'I'm doing it for Lady Arbella,' said Alice, 'and for those who love her. I lost someone I loved. It hurts to think of others going through the same torment.'

Tom lowered his head, feeling somewhat chastened.

The door opened and Robert Poley emerged, along with the gaoler. Poley was as tall and thin as the gaoler was short and wide. They made an odd-looking pair.

'Everything is arranged,' Poley said to Tom and Alice. 'Mr Kendrick here has been made aware of the situation. He and his guards will step in and protect you should Watson turn violent. For this service, he has been paid handsomely with treasury funds.' With a wince, he added: 'Some might say a little too handsomely.'

Kendrick smiled, displaying a set of ruined teeth, one of which glinted gold. He patted the fat purse hanging from his belt. 'I thank you most heartily, Mr Poley, sir.' Then he fixed his watery, bloodshot gaze upon Tom and Alice. 'Don't expect any favoured treatment once you're in there,' he warned them. 'If Watson is to believe you is inmates of my gaol, I can't treat you no different from the rest.'

Tom nodded, cringing at the man's onion breath, and wishing more than ever he could be back in the sanctuary of York House.

'Remember your cover stories,' said Poley. 'You're both Catholic recusants…'

'Sorry, what's a recusant again?' asked Tom.

Poley sighed and shook his head. 'It's a Catholic who refuses to attend Church of England services. You've been imprisoned here for not paying your fines after failing to attend service at your local church.' He handed them each a small leather purse of coins. 'This is to pay for food, candles and bedding while you're in there.'

'Nuffing in the Clink comes free,' chuckled Kendrick, treating them to another flash of his gold tooth.

'Now you'll need some sort of code phrase to let Mr Kendrick know when you're ready to be released,' said Poley. 'Any suggestions? Something short and pithy would be best…'

'The quality of mercy is not strain'd,' said Alice.

'What?' frowned Poley.

She continued: 'It droppeth as the gentle rain from heaven upon the place beneath: it is twice blest; it blesseth him that gives and him that takes…'

'Alright, alright, that's enough of that,' interjected Poley. 'I said "short and pithy", didn't I? Where does it come from anyway?'

'It was written by a friend of mine,' said Alice, 'from a play he wrote called *The Merchant of Venice*. It's one of my favourite passages, and I was due to perform it tomorrow – except your master had other ideas.'

'Well, you could use the first bit,' said Poley. 'The quality of er…'

'…mercy is not strained,' finished Alice.

'Will you remember that, Mr Kendrick?' asked Poley.

'Aye,' nodded the bewildered gaoler, 'though I've not the first clue what it means.'

'Well, good luck, the pair of you,' said Poley, attempting an encouraging grin.

Reluctantly, Tom began following Kendrick and Alice through the door.

'Just one more thing,' said Poley, tugging Tom aside. He handed him a set of beads on a string with a crucifix at one end. 'Rosary beads,' explained Poley. 'I could only get hold of one set. You take them – they'll add credence to your cover story.'

Tom thanked him dully and pocketed them, before slipping through the closing door into the prison. His senses were immediately assaulted by an overpowering stench of damp walls, rancid food and sour sweat. Trying not to gag, he concentrated on breathing through his mouth. Kendrick took a torch from a wall bracket and began leading them down some steps and along a corridor of age-blackened stone walls lined with iron-barred doors leading to cells. Guards with heavy keys dangling from their belts were seated on stools outside the cells at regular intervals along the corridor.

Desperate-looking men with large eyes and sunken cheeks stared up at them from the cells. They sat or lay upon piles of dirty straw – four or five to a cell. They had manacles around their ankles or wrists attached to a chain bolted to the wall – like dogs kept on a leash.

One or two had the energy to crawl to their cell door as Kendrick went by, thrusting their hands between the bars and groaning for food or water. Kendrick ignored them. A bored-looking guard stood up and bashed his cudgel against the bars, forcing them to withdraw their hands.

'They be the lowest of the low,' Kendrick grunted to Tom and Alice. 'They get nuffing from us cos they got no money. Once a day I'll let the priest in with his alms-basket and he can chuck 'em a few scraps. Or they might get sumfing through the grates.'

'The grates?' queried Alice.

Kendrick pointed at the rectangles of parallel iron bars set in the ceilings of the cells, letting in light and air from above. 'If they is lucky, someone in the street up there'll drop a crust of bread or a coin through the bars. But most of 'em ain't very lucky. We get about thirty deaths a year here, on average...'

Tom felt a rising nausea in his stomach. He kept his gaze straight ahead, trying to avoid the sight of those desperate eyes and the hands reaching through the bars. Although he knew he and Alice were not criminals and would not be staying here long, a creeping sense of hopelessness and dejection stole through him, sapping his strength. He dreaded facing Watson, and doubted he had the cunning or the quickness of mind to fool such a man into spilling his secrets. He rubbed the prayer beads in his pocket. Strangely, this seemed to calm him.

Further along the corridor, the cells became noticeably emptier and more spacious, with just two or three inmates per cell. They had rushlights on the wall, and were furnished with mattresses and even chairs and a table. The prisoners were better dressed and looked reasonably well fed. They did not wear manacles or leg irons.

'Good morrow, Mr Kendrick,' someone shouted.

'Good morrow to you, sir,' the gaoler replied. To Tom and Alice, he said: 'These be my paying customers. They get good treatment, so long as they keep up their payments.'

He stopped at the door of one of these cells. It contained just one inmate, who was facing away from them in a kneeling position, muttering a prayer beneath a crucifix that hung on the wall.

'Father Watson!' called Kendrick.

Chapter 6

The Perfect Assassin

BRADENSTOKE HALL, 1ST MAY 1603

Robert Catesby removed his hat and studied the hole. Then he looked at Richard and said: 'I've never seen you before in my life, young man.' He spoke softly, but there was a dangerous edge to his voice.

'That hole dates back to the Essex Rebellion, doesn't it?' said Markham.

'Aye,' said Catesby. He was standing perfectly still, watching Richard like a cat waiting to pounce on its prey. But Markham's gaze kept wandering, and he shifted restlessly from foot to foot. Richard noticed Markham glancing at a sword hanging on the wall near the hearth. *Was his host seriously thinking of attacking him?*

'Now I think about it,' said Markham, 'perhaps that robber *did* look a little like you, old fellow.'

Catesby shot an irritated look in Markham's direction, and suddenly Richard knew they were both lying. He also knew with equal certainty that he lacked the skill with words to prove this. Yet he could not let the matter drop. He *had* to know what was going on.

His only choice was to force the truth out of them. He was still fast and strong, even after weeks of living comfortably here as Markham's guest. Perhaps he had a chance…

Before he'd even properly decided upon a plan, Richard's body sprang into action. He made a dive for the sword on the wall, plucking it from its hook and spinning towards Catesby, who was reaching for his flintlock. Before Catesby could free the firearm from its holster, the point of Richard's sword jabbed the skin of his neck.

Animal instinct had driven Richard to target the more dangerous of the two men. Though Markham was also a soldier by background, Richard sensed a softness in him that made him less of a threat.

Catesby took a step back. His expression remained disturbingly calm and self-confident. Richard extended his reach so the sword tip remained in stabbing distance of Catesby's neck.

'Put the sword down, Richard,' ordered Markham,

trying and not quite managing to sound relaxed.

'First tell me the truth.'

'Perhaps you should call one of your guards, Markham,' suggested Catesby.

'I'll kill you if he does,' said Richard, meeting Catesby's gaze with a steely one of his own.

'Please, Richard,' said Markham, edging slowly towards him.

'One step closer and your friend dies,' said Richard, surprised at his own calmness.

Markham's shoulders slumped. 'Alright,' he said. 'Put the sword down and we'll tell you everything.'

'Markham, you bootless, boil-brained canker-blossom!' Catesby scowled.

Markham sank into a chair and put his head in his hands. 'It's alright, Robert,' he sighed. 'We owe him the truth.'

Catesby's eyes blazed with frustration. 'Alright,' he snapped. 'Put down your sword, you young clot-pole. I'll tell you what you want to know – although you'll be taking this knowledge with you to the grave, which may be sooner than you think.'

Richard swallowed. *Did he really want to know this? Aye! He was sick of living in ignorance.* 'First throw aside your pistol,' he said.

With a grimace, Catesby took out the long wood-and-iron flintlock and slid it across the floor tiles.

Richard lowered his sword, but did not discard it. 'Speak!' he demanded.

Catesby studied his hat, tracing the hole from Richard's arrow with his finger. 'You're right,' he said. 'It was me in the forest that day, robbing Markham.' Glancing up at Markham, he added: 'I didn't think the boy would recognise me.'

'He's observant,' muttered Markham. 'We always knew that.'

Always knew...? Richard was stunned by this remark.

'Why would you rob your friend?' he asked.

Catesby sighed. 'It was a set-up. We *wanted* you to intervene. We had to find a way to bring you back here without you suspecting anything.'

Richard's jaw went slack. *A set-up*?

'Tell it from the beginning, Robert,' said Markham. 'You need to start in 1601.'

'Very well,' frowned Catesby. 'As you know, Markham and I were involved in the Essex Uprising that year. I was looking to recruit an assassin – someone who could kill silently from range.'

'An archer,' said Markham.

'An archer,' nodded Catesby. 'I was tipped off by one of my associates, a young player named Edmund Squires. He told me about you and your talent with a bow and arrow. He said you went out hunting in the woods around Camberwell on your free days...'

'Wait,' said Richard, struggling to keep up. 'How did this Edmund Squires know about me?'

'Because you were a player, too. You and Squires worked for a troupe called the Chamberlain's Men.'

Richard almost dropped his sword in surprise. 'I was a… a player, on the stage?' He recalled his dream the night before – or was it a memory?

'Aye. You performed regularly at a playhouse called the Globe.'

'And where was that?'

'In Southwark – London.'

Richard's mouth fell open. 'So how did I end up in the Forest of Arden?'

'There hangs a tale,' chuckled Markham.

'I followed you on one of your jaunts into Camberwell,' said Catesby. 'I saw what a fine shot you were, but I needed something more than bowmanship for my assassin – I needed nerves of steel. So I devised a test for you. I told Squires to send you to a man named Jasper Scrope, and deliver him a message. Scrope was another assassin – a ruthless man, made fearless by the fact that he was dying from consumption. I planned to use him as part of the Essex Rebellion. He was a frightening fellow to encounter in the flesh, and he lived in a very rough part of town. I sent you there to deliver the message to him as a test of your character.'

'And did I deliver the message?'

'Aye,' said Markham. 'But the message was wrong – it very nearly cost you your life.'

'What do you mean?'

'My plan had been to recruit you as soon as you completed the mission,' said Catesby. 'I wanted Scrope to capture and hold you in his room until I could get there myself and talk to you. So I told Squires to end the communiqué with the words: *Capture deliverer of this message*. But Squires, either through error or design, instead wrote: *Kill deliverer of this message.*'

'I believe he was a rival of yours in the Chamberlain's Men,' said Markham. 'You were both competing to become hired men. Squires may have seen this as an opportunity to get rid of you.'

'By good fortune I arrived just before Scrope killed you,' said Catesby. 'But not before he delivered a severe blow to your head. After a while, you awoke, but without any memory of who you were. I couldn't tell if you'd be of any use to me. So I took you up here, to the Forest of Arden, to see if you could survive on your own. I kept watch on you, and quickly saw that you'd lost none of your skills. You could move silently, and shoot with accuracy. You remained the perfect assassin.' Richard's grip on the sword tightened. 'You used me! You've been using me all along.'

'Aye,' nodded Catesby. 'I kept watch over you for more than two years. In all that time, you never saw me once – but you were aware of me, and you feared me, which was good.'

'The Evil One,' murmured Richard, eyes widening in shock. '*You* are the Evil One.'

Catesby chuckled. 'Nay, that part you have wrong. I've spent my life fighting *against* evil. And the chance has now arisen for us to strike a mortal blow against the heathens who rule over us. That's why we had to bring you in from the forest. We staged the bandit attack, knowing that you were watching and would act to protect Markham. I wore protective mail under my clothing that day, but I need not have. Your compassion and skill meant I was never in danger.

That you have a gift, Richard Fletcher, is beyond doubt. All that remains to be seen is whether you have the spirit and the grit to use that gift to do God's work.'

Richard tried to breathe, but it was difficult. A veil had been lifted from his eyes, and it revealed a terrible reality. He raised the sword so it was pointing at Catesby's chest. The tip shook as he said: 'For all your talk of God's work, you are a cruel man, Mr Catesby. What kind of god would lead you to destroy someone's life, remove him from his friends and family, watch him as he endures months of fear, hunger and loneliness in a forest. What kind of god would make you do that? No god that I could ever serve! Do not ask me again to do his work.'

Hearing this, Catesby became very flushed. His lips turned pale and his eyes glittered with rage, but he said nothing.

'We have treated you very badly, it's true,' said Markham. 'But if you perform this deed for us, I promise that you will be allowed to go back to your family.'

Richard turned in contempt towards his host. 'Never!' he said. 'I'd sooner return to the forest.'

As he said this, he felt a sharp blow to his hand. Catesby had kicked the sword from his grasp.

The weapon clattered to the floor. Richard reached for it, but Catesby was quicker. He scooped it up, at the same time knocking Richard backwards with his elbow so that he fell hard against the table. When Richard looked up, it was to see the sharp end of the sword pointing at his chin, and Catesby smirking at him.

'You're going nowhere, Fletcher,' Catesby said. 'It would have been better for you if you hadn't forced us to tell you the truth – but now you know it, we can never let you go, and Markham was wrong to suggest otherwise. You're one of us now, whether you like it or not, and you'll do exactly what you're told.'

Chapter 7

Come to Me, My Lambs

THE CLINK, 1ST MAY 1603

The skin on the back of Tom's neck tingled on hearing the name 'Father Watson'. He was almost sure his nervousness would be their undoing – the priest would know instantly that he was a spy. Watson twisted to face them. He was a large, solidly built man of middle age with a ruddy complexion and cropped grey hair that stuck up from his head like iron filings in one of Sir Francis's magnetism experiments.

'God ye good den, Mr Kendrick,' he said in a slow, deep voice, while scrutinizing Tom and Alice.

'I'm putting these two in with you, Father,' said Kendrick, as a guard unlocked the cell door.

'I thought we agreed no company, Mr Kendrick. Or is my money not good enough for you these days.'

'As I says to you before, Father, I is happy to oblige you on this, so long as we don't get full. We is now full, so we has to put these two in here with you.'

Alice and Tom filed into the cell.

'Bedding, candles and an evening meal will cost you a shilling each,' said Kendrick.

After accepting their coins, he sauntered away with a satisfied smile, and the cell door clanged shut.

Watson squinted at them. 'By the looks of you, I'd say you were in for petty thieving. Cut-purses or coney-catchers are you?'

'Nay, recusants,' said Alice.

Watson's face changed when he heard this. His eyebrows rose and his ears seemed to prick up, almost like a cat's. 'Recusants...? Is this some attempt to curry favour with me? You're no recusants. You're not even Catholic.'

'We are, sir,' insisted Tom, trying to keep the tremor out of his voice.

Watson rose to his feet, his mouth twisted to a cruel slant. 'Then it must be by the grace of God you have come here,' he said sarcastically. Holding out his arms, he invited them to approach: 'Come to me, my lambs.'

Frightened, but realising they had little choice but to play the part assigned to them, Tom and Alice came closer and allowed themselves to be embraced by the priest.

Watson's bony hand clutched Tom's shoulder far too tightly for comfort.

'Let us pray and give thanks for this miracle,' the priest grunted, forcing them down onto their knees.

Kneeling between them before his makeshift altar, Watson released his grip on their shoulders and clasped his hands together. In his deep voice, he intoned the words of a prayer: *'Anima Christi, sanctifica me. Corpus Christi, salva me. Sanguis Christi, inebria me. Aqua lateris Christi, lava me...'* After several lines of this, he lapsed into silence.

Tom, unused to hearing prayers in Latin, belatedly realised it had ended and gabbled: 'Amen'. Alice was half a second slower.

Watson gave her a sly glance. 'Now let's say the Lord's Prayer, *together*,' he purred. *'Pater Noster, qui es in caelis...'*

When Tom and Alice failed to join in, Watson stopped and looked at each of them in turn, his lips curled in a sneer. 'Come now, my lambs, don't be shy. Surely, you know *this* one.'

Of course they both knew the Lord's Prayer – but in English, as it was recited in Anglican churches.

'I'm sorry, Father,' said Alice. 'It's... It's been so long since we celebrated mass...'

'But Catholic children absorb the Lord's Prayer with their mother's milk,' said Watson. And the soft, smiling tone faded from his voice. 'You're liars, both of you,' he growled. 'You're about as Catholic as the king of England.'

Tom kept his eyes shut, hands pressed tightly together. He remembered hearing the Latin version of the prayer before, more than two years ago in the courtyard at Essex House, where Catholic soldiers had gathered to fight for his former master. If only he could remember the words...

Watson's fingers were, once again, squeezing hard into his shoulder, making it impossible to think.

'You're here for a reason,' said the priest. 'Spies aren't you? Kendrick must have put you up to this, trying to ingratiate himself with the king. Well, Kendrick can't hear you now! Round about now, he'll be getting drunk down at the Boar's Head. Which means you're mine to do with as I please...'

The pain in Tom's shoulder had become so intense, he couldn't help but groan. He heard Alice catch her breath in an audible gasp. The priest had fingers like iron.

'Scream all you like, the guards won't come,' snarled Watson. 'Kendrick doesn't know it, but I've paid them to ignore what goes on in this cell.'

So now they were at Watson's mercy! Tom inwardly cursed Cecil for exposing them to this monster.

Abruptly, Watson pushed them forwards, shoving their heads to the floor. 'Confess!' he growled. 'Confess to what you are!'

Tom's forehead and nose were pressed mercilessly against the cold stone, as Watson's hand pushed down on the back of his head. In this uncomfortable position, the words he'd been trying to recall suddenly and unexpectedly began to pour out of him: *'Sanctificetur nomen tuum. Adveniat regnum tuum. Fiat voluntas tua, sicut in caelo et in terra.'* His voice sounded muffled, even in his own ears, yet he was sure the words were audible. Even so, the pressure of Watson's hand did not relinquish. *'Panem nostrum quotidianum da nobis hodie, et dimitte nobis debita nostra, sicut et nos dimittimus debitoribus nostris. Et ne nos inducas in tentationem, sed libera nos a malo. Amen.'*

He was amazed the Latin had come back to him, word for word. He waited tensely for Watson to react. Eventually, the crushing force of the priest's grip eased, and he and Alice were allowed to rise again into a kneeling position. Tom could sense Alice staring at him incredulously, but he didn't dare meet her eyes. Instead, he meditated piously upon the crucifix on the wall in front of them.

It was around then that a guard came in with their bedding and candles. Tom guessed the guard had been hiding just out of sight, waiting for Watson to stop hurting them before making his appearance. A little later, another guard arrived with food from the prison kitchen – bread and pottage made from bacon, oats and cabbage.

Watson unexpectedly invited Tom and Alice to join him at the table for their evening meal. The priest didn't admit that he had been wrong about them, yet his demeanour was definitely more friendly. He even told them his story.

'My parents sent me to France at the age of sixteen,' Watson said between slurps of his pottage. 'After eleven years of study, I was ordained a priest. I returned to England in 1586 in a missionary role, encouraging the faithful and ministering to their spiritual needs. For the last sixteen years I have lived a life in the shadows, always on the move, celebrating secret masses, hiding for days on end in cramped priest holes, trying to stay one step ahead of the pursuivants. I have been tortured and imprisoned more times than I can remember.' Watson chewed forcefully on the rind of some bacon. 'It's made me what I am – hard. That is the only way I can survive and do the Lord's work. I have no friends. Friends soften you. Friends betray you. My only friend is Our Lord Jesus Christ.'

He lapsed into silence.

'Did… Did you ever think about how we could change this state of affairs?' asked Alice.

Watson stared at her. 'What do you mean?' he asked slowly.

'Instead of living in fear, as we do, we could try and restore England to the True Faith?'

The priest's eyes narrowed, and Tom had difficulty swallowing his bread. Alice was playing a dangerous game.

'You mean bring down the government?' Watson asked.

Alice shrugged. 'Something like that,' she said innocently.

Watson continued to stare at her, the food on his spoon forgotten, and Tom began to fear that the priest was about to become violent again. Eventually, he shovelled the oats and cabbage into his mouth. After a lot of noisy, wet chewing, he said: 'No, I've never thought about anything like that.'

That night, Tom twisted and turned on his thin mattress, unable to sleep. The air was stuffy and filled with unpleasant odours. Snores and guttural groans crept in from the other cells, along with the faint scufflings of rats in the straw. He spent long moments wishing himself back in his clean and comfortable attic room at York House, and even longer moments wishing terrible maladies upon the Beagle for forcing him to spend time in this hellish place.

At length, when he'd become exhausted of such thoughts, he decided to try and use the time more constructively to devise a strategy for dealing with Father Watson. A patient approach, he decided, was best. He would need to win the man's trust before carefully probing him for information. Alice had been far too hasty in her questioning this evening. A more subtle approach was called for, and that, sadly, might take some days.

The sound of approaching footsteps interrupted these thoughts. A bulky shadow loomed out of the darkness. A pale hint of moonlight seeping through the grate in the ceiling revealed a face.

Watson!

Tom quailed at the sight of him. He squashed himself against the wall.

What was he doing? Had he come to murder him?

'Boy?' came Watson's low voice.

'Wh-What?' Tom managed.

The priest bent over him. His nasal breathing was heavy and loud. 'Your stay in the Clink will be short, I'm guessing?' he whispered.

'I–I…' Tom could barely get his words out. *What was the man saying? That he'd be dead by morning?*

'Your crime is a petty one,' continued Watson in his low rumble. 'Refusal to go to the heretical church, am I right?'

'Aye,' gasped Tom.

Watson hushed him with a finger to his lips and a surreptitious glance towards Alice's bed.

Why was he so concerned not to wake her?

'That means you'll be out soon enough,' whispered Watson.

'I suppose so,' said Tom more quietly.

Watson pulled a long, rolled-up strip of paper from his pocket. 'I want to entrust this to you, boy. It's a message that needs to go to someone I know – a soldier named Sir Griffin Markham.' He dangled the narrow parchment ribbon close to Tom's face. Tom reached up to take it, and Watson seemed about to hand it to him, but then he paused, his face creased with sudden doubts. 'Why should I trust you?'

'You *must* trust me!' breathed Tom. He *had* to get hold of that message. It could lead them straight to Lady Arbella.

Watson nodded towards Alice. 'But you came in here with *that* one, who doesn't know the Lord's Prayer and who tried to goad me into speaking of my... activities.'

'He...'

'He's a spy, isn't he? Tell the truth!'

'No, of course he isn't a spy.'

'How do you know that?' Watson's eyes blazed into Tom's. 'How well do you even know him?'

Tom could feel his lips trembling as he tried to come up with something that would satisfy the mistrustful priest. 'N-Not so well, but...'

'Then he *might* be... For all you know he *might* be a spy, sent here by Kendrick.'

'He's not a spy!' hissed Tom, frightened now of what Watson had in mind for Alice.

'Do you swear it?'

'Of course I do!'

Watson leaned back on his haunches, his expression disappointed. 'Then I cannot trust you,' he said, repocketing the roll of paper. 'If you are prepared to defend this boy you hardly know – this boy who doesn't know the most familiar prayers of the Tridentine Mass – then what am I to conclude? Are you in league with him?'

'Of course not,' gabbled Tom, feeling pinned down by the priest's iron stare. 'I'm not in league with anyone.' Desperate to claw his way back into Watson's trust, he tugged the rosary beads from his pocket. He held them out so he could see them. 'I will deliver your message,' Tom vowed. 'You have to trust me.'

Watson squinted at the beads, and then at him. 'Why should I, when you won't even admit that your companion might be a spy?'

The message might be gold dust to Cecil, but if the price was denouncing Alice, Tom wasn't prepared to pay it. But was a middle way possible?

'Swear to me first that you won't harm Adam,' he said.

'What?' frothed Watson.

'If you swear in God's name you won't hurt him... I'll tell you what you want to hear.'

'Why do you care what happens to him?'

'Because we're friends. We may not know each other very well, but I like him and I fear what you might do to him.'

Watson growled, 'Very well! I swear by the Lord God he'll be safe while he's under this roof.'

Tom nodded, satisfied. 'Then it's true, I cannot say for sure that he's not a spy.' As he said this, he glanced over to where Alice lay and was shocked to see that her eyes were open. She'd been listening to everything...

Chapter 8

Voices from the Hearth

BRADENSTOKE HALL, 1ST MAY 1603

'Call your guards, Markham,' said Catesby, keeping his eyes, and his sword, firmly trained upon Richard.

A rueful-looking Markham did so, and before long Richard found himself being steered from the room by two armoured men bearing halberds. 'Fear not, Richard,' Markham called after him. 'We will speak again about this.'

Richard was escorted to a room on the upper storey of the east wing. One of the guards lit a candle, illuminating a small, plain chamber furnished with a simple bed and no other furniture. A single recessed window offered a view of the moat and the forest beyond, though it was by now too dark outside to see much. The guards departed the room, closing the door behind them, and Richard heard the sound of a key being turned in the lock. He listened for the sound of the guards' footsteps moving back up the corridor, but couldn't hear them. The guards were staying put outside his door. If he needed confirmation that his status had changed, this was it: he was now a prisoner at Bradenstoke Hall.

Jake Heathcock had been right. The people here were not what they seemed. He'd been lured to this house like a rabbit into a trap, to help them carry out some murderous deed. But at least he now knew the truth – he was no longer under any illusion about why he was here.

Richard picked up the candle by the bed and wandered over to the small hearth set in the long left-hand wall. A fire would be pleasant – more for its light than heat, as it was a mild night. Yet disappointingly, no kindling had been provided. Indeed, the interior of the fireplace was surprisingly shallow, with the rear wall set mere inches back from the grate. Puzzled, he felt about for the chimney opening at the top and could not find it. A false fireplace. *How very odd!*

Shrugging, Richard got back to his feet and went instead to the window, which he unbolted and threw open. Beneath him was a sheer drop of thirty feet to the inky waters of the moat. No easy escape that way!

After a moment spent pondering the view, he went and lay down on the bed. He tried to process what had happened this evening, and all the things he had learned. So he had been a player performing on a stage in London. Such a life was hard to imagine. Did he have family in London then? A mother and father? Brothers and sisters? He couldn't remember anyone.

Yet in a dream he'd had recently – and dreams were perhaps the only way he had of accessing his buried memories – he'd been accompanied by a girl. That had been strange enough, because in all his other dreams he'd been alone. He couldn't remember anything about this girl – who she was, what she looked like, her age (though he had the sense she was younger than him). He only remembered she was there, walking beside him, and he felt protective towards her. They were walking through the forest, feeling hungry, when they came upon a high wall. On the other side of the wall, there was food – somehow they both knew this. But getting hold of it was difficult and dangerous. The wall was high. There were guards. He was worried about letting the girl go over the wall, but before he could stop her she was climbing up it, clambering right over the top...

Richard was interrupted in these contemplations by a faint noise from outside. It sounded like someone arriving at the house. He leapt up from the bed and ran over to the casement. By leaning out of the window and craning his neck as far as he could to his left, he was able to see the arrival of a coach and horses. It was crossing the double-arched bridge that spanned the moat, heading for the gatehouse. He wondered if this was 'the lady' Markham and Catesby had spoken of earlier. Was she part of their plan to 'strike a mortal blow against the heathens'?

The coach passed into the gatehouse and beyond Richard's view. He remained at the window, observing the pink afterglow of the sunset above the billowing mass of dark trees. If only he could be back there now, enjoying the freedom of the forest. He no longer had any need to fear the Evil One, for now he knew he was mortal, and killable. Yet Catesby had managed to evade discovery for a very long time – he must be adept at the arts of concealment and surveillance. If Richard *did* manage to escape, he was sure Catesby would come after him and try and hunt him down. Well, two could play at that game. Richard knew all about stalking prey. Catesby would have to be careful that the hunter did not become the hunted.

He contemplated the darkly gleaming moat beneath him. Could he survive a jump from this height? What if the water was shallow there? The fall could be fatal. And if he *did* survive, would he be able to swim to the far side? He didn't know if he could swim at all. The forest streams he had forded had never been deeper than his waist. Yet, he'd surprised himself with his horse-riding ability. Maybe he could swim, too. Perhaps it would be better to die in the attempt than remain locked up here…

A faint light flared in the darkness to his left. Richard leaned out to see what was going on. A candle was flickering in a nearby window, just before the great jutting side wall of the gatehouse. Someone had come into the room next to his. The window opened. Briefly, he glimpsed a small, pale hand on the glass – a woman's hand. So the lady *had* arrived, and gone straight to her bedchamber. But why had she been taken here to the dismal east wing, with guards in its corridor? Why not to the far more comfortable west wing?

Was she a prisoner, too?

If only he could communicate with her. Perhaps together they could devise a plan to escape. He examined the wall directly beneath his window, searching for any sign of a ledge or foothold that could carry him across to her room. There was none. The wall was entirely smooth.

Frustrated, he went and seated himself on the bed. As he sat there pondering what to do next, he heard a faint noise – it sounded like low voices murmuring. At first he assumed it was the guards outside the room, but then he realised that the voices weren't coming from that direction, they were coming from the wall. In fact, they seemed to be emerging from the hearth.

He crept closer. Crouching down, he placed his ear next to the brickwork at the back of the fireplace. A young woman was speaking very faintly, her voice somehow seeping out of the bricks.

'When can I see Edward?' she asked.

'Edward?' replied an even more muffled male voice
– it sounded like Markham.

'Edward Seymour – the man I am to marry. I know
he planned this… the rescue from Hardwick Hall. It's
all so very exciting. I can't wait to see him.'

Markham, if it was him, said something indistinct.
The woman replied angrily: 'Not Edward? I refuse to
believe that! Prithee, take me to him at once!'

The man now spoke for a long time, but Richard
could not make out more than a few phrases: *brought
here for your own safety … he is a usurper … you are the
rightful heir …*

The lady was silent through all this. When the man
finished speaking, Richard heard a door squeak open
and then closed. After that, there was silence, apart
from the faint sound of the lady sobbing.

Chapter 9

The Sign of the Fish

SOUTHWARK, 2ND MAY 1603

Tom felt terrible. He'd betrayed Alice, his closest friend. Worse, Alice knew this. Her eyes were closed now, but a moment ago they'd been open, and she'd heard him tell William Watson, the violent, unstable priest, that she might be a spy. Watson had promised him she'd be safe, but could he trust him? The man was a fanatic, after all, who divided the world between good and evil, and he was sure to have placed Alice on the evil side of the line. What were those words she'd said outside the prison?

The quality of mercy is not strain'd, it droppeth as the gentle rain from heaven upon the place beneath: it is twice blest; It blesseth him that gives and him that takes...

Tom stared up at the priest with his iron-filing hair and his calm grey eyes. This man would not understand such sentiments. He probably saw mercy as weakness. 'I have no friends,' he'd told them. 'Friends soften you.' Well, maybe it was a good thing they did. Maybe he needed friends to soften his cruel streak, to teach him about mercy. If such a ruthless man was involved in the kidnap of Lady Arbella and the plot to overthrow James, then the kingdom was truly in jeopardy. He had to be stopped.

'I've told you what you want to hear,' said Tom through gritted teeth.

'Aye,' growled Watson. 'That you have.'

'Now you must trust me.'

'Must I?'

Watson put his hand back in his pocket, but instead of pulling out the message, he drew out a small knife in a leather scabbard. The blade, when he revealed it, gleamed with a cold light. It was short and extremely sharp. Tom shrank from it, but Watson seized hold of his right arm. Tom struggled desperately as the priest yanked up the sleeve of his shirt, but he was powerless – the man was too strong. Watson pinned Tom's wrist to the mattress, and lowered the pointed tip of his knife towards his arm.

'No!' cried Tom. 'Get off me!'

Behind Watson's shoulder, Tom saw Alice sit bolt upright in her bed, eyes wide as she took in what was happening. She rose swiftly and silently from her mattress and began creeping towards Watson. She picked up a wooden bowl containing the dregs of pottage, to use as a weapon. Tom, meanwhile, was using all his strength to try and prise himself free of Watson's powerful grip, but he could not prevent the knife tip moving ever closer to his forearm. Alice raised the bowl, intending to bring it crashing down on Watson's head, but before she could do so, Watson jerked back the elbow of his right hand, hard, straight into her knee.

Alice cried out. She lost her balance, falling backwards and hitting her head against the table. The bowl fell with a clatter. As Tom was taking this in, a terrible pain seared his arm. The blade had begun to cut. He screamed as Watson sliced quickly in a shallow, curved line through his skin. Dark blood spilled from the gash. Watson cut a two inch arc before adjusting the knife's position and cutting again in another curve, the mirror image of the first. Tom choked with horror as he watched the second line form, intersecting with the first at one end. More blood flowed. Watson swiftly tugged the bandanna from his neck and clamped it to the wound.

'Hold it there until the bleeding stops,' he ordered.

'Wh-What… What did you do that for?' whimpered Tom.

'It's my symbol,' grunted Watson. 'A fish. Sir Griffin Markham will see it, and he'll know I sent you. You're one of us now, boy.'

Watson pulled out the long thin scrap of paper with the message for Markham, and stuffed it into Tom's pocket.

Tom blinked back tears of pain as he pressed the bandanna tightly to his arm. 'By God, you could have told me what you were doing!' he gasped. 'I thought you were going to kill me.'

Watson whispered to him: 'He lives in a moated manor house called Bradenstoke Hall in the Forest of Arden in Warwickshire. Make sure it reaches him.'

'I will,' wheezed Tom. He saw Alice climbing slowly back to her feet, looking very groggy. 'Are you alright?' he called to her.

Alice rubbed her head and nodded. 'What did you do to him?' she asked Watson.

He turned on her and spat: 'None of your concern, boy. Go back to bed.' To Tom he murmured: 'You breathe a word of this to your friend, and I'll kill you both, y'hear?'

'I understand,' said Tom, who was finding it hard to focus on anything beyond the pain in his arm.

'Now get some rest,' said Watson as he shambled off to his bed.

Tom turned his face to the wall, shivering from the aftershock of his ordeal. Sleep came, eventually, and it was filled with frightening, nonsensical dreams in which he was being chased by a man in priestly robes with the head of a fish and giant magnets for hands, who kept sucking him backwards into his cold, painful embrace.

Grim, grey bars of daylight leaking in from the street above awoke him. The pain in his arm had subsided. The bandanna had become stuck to the wound. Tenderly, he pulled it away. Scabs were forming over the two curved cuts. The cuts joined on one side, forming the 'mouth' of the fish, and they crossed on the other side, with the two short ends forming the fish's 'tail'. As Father Watson had intended, it would form a scar that would always be with him. *You're one of us now, boy!*

A guard arrived with acorn bread and water. This time, to Tom's relief, Watson did not invite his cell mates to join him at the table. Without saying a word to either of them, Watson tossed a corner of the loaf in his direction, and another one towards Alice. Tom glanced across at her, but she didn't look up. Presently, Mr Kendrick arrived on his morning inspection. He was red-nosed and a little unsteady on his feet after what must have been a jolly night at the Boar's Head.

'All well?' he asked them through the bars of their cell door.

'The quality of mercy is not strain'd,' Tom said to him.

Watson looked up sharply. 'Eh? What was that?'

Tom shuddered at his stare. Why couldn't Alice have chosen a less conspicuous phrase – something like: 'Zounds! What an uncomfortable mattress. I barely got a wink of sleep.' That would have served them so much better.

'It's j-just something I always say,' Tom quavered, 'when…'

'When what?' demanded Watson.

Tom was painfully aware that his mouth was opening and closing, but no words were coming out.

'Whenever someone says "all well",' said Alice. 'He really is a very odd person, aren't you, Tom?'

'Aye,' muttered Tom. 'That I am.'

Watson wrinkled his nose. 'The quality of mercy is not strange... Sounds heretical to me. What do you mean by it?'

'Never you mind what he means!' chuckled Kendrick. 'I'm sure he don't mean nuffing. It's just sumfing he says is all. Like an affliction. I say "all well", and then he says them words... Anon, gentlemen. I shall see you all again tomorrow.'

With that, he went on his way.

Of course Kendrick couldn't let them out then and there – that would look too suspicious. All the same, Tom was nervous. What if Kendrick had also been bribed by Father Watson? He might have accepted Poley's money while planning all along to leave them in the sadistic hands of the priest.

The hours that followed were a miserable combination of nerve-wracking and tedious. Tom occupied the time by either sitting on his mattress or pacing around his corner of the cell. A bowl of cold water was brought in for them to wash with, and a bucket to relieve themselves in.

Watson used the 'facilities' first. Tom then signalled

to Alice to go next, and he faced the wall to give her some privacy. It was the only time they communicated. Apart from that, Alice refused to meet his eye, even when Watson was at prayer. He realised she had every reason to be angry with him for 'betraying' her, but couldn't she see he had no choice? He'd had to get hold of that note – the note that would lead them to Lady Arbella, who Alice had seemed so keen to save. And did she have no sympathy for what *he'd* had to go through in pursuit of that goal? He was scarred for life! *And* he'd made Watson promise not to hurt her. What more could he have done?

Tom had worked himself up into quite a resentful state by the time the cell door finally squeaked open and a guard told him he could leave. But self-pity quickly changed to alarm when he realised Alice wasn't being released with him. He tried to convince himself this was a good thing – if they left together, it might reignite Watson's suspicions that they were in league. Yet he couldn't help feeling extremely apprehensive about leaving Alice alone with him. Tom wished he could catch her eye, just to reassure her, yet even at this stage she wouldn't look at him. But Watson did. As Tom got up to leave, the priest started staring at him, and his gaze was full of dark warnings. *Deliver the message*, he seemed to be saying, *and don't even think about betraying me!*

Tom found Kendrick counting his money in a little office at the top of the steps. 'You must let Adam out, too,' Tom told him. 'He's not safe in there with that man.'

Kendrick hushed him with a gesture as he continued tallying his coins. Finally he looked up. 'He didn't say none of them words,' he said.

'He *can't!*' cried Tom. 'You saw how Watson looked at me when I said that phrase. If Adam comes out with the same thing, he'll know something's up.'

'Alright, alright,' snorted the gaoler. 'But Poley told me to stagger the releases. I'll let 'im out before the end of the day, never you mind.'

Tom took a deep breath, trying to remain calm. 'Very well. But please place a guard on the cell at all times. And make sure it's someone you trust. Watson's been bribing some of them to close their eyes to what goes on in his cell.'

Kendrick looked thunderstruck. 'Only one man takes bribes in this establishment and that's me!'

'Very well then, here you are!' glowered Tom, handing him his leather purse full of coins.

Kendrick's eyes lit up as he snatched up the purse.

'For that,' said Tom, 'I want your solemn vow that you will personally keep watch over the cell until you see fit to release him.'

'You have it,' purred Kendrick as he opened up the purse and let the coins pour onto the table.

The air in the street outside was far from sweet-smelling, carrying with it strong hints of the meat market and the putrid river. Even so, it was a hundred times fresher than the air Tom had had to endure in the Clink, and he greedily filled his lungs with it.

He wanted more than anything to look at the message Watson had given him, but first he needed to find somewhere more private. He decided to head to the Anchor, a nearby riverside tavern. There he could await Alice's release, and hopefully find a secluded corner to study the message. As he made his way there, Tom noticed the streets were unusually quiet. He had expected to encounter crowds heading west towards the Globe and the other centres of entertainment in Bankside, but there were very few people about, and those there were walked quickly, keeping their heads down.

The loud squeak of a cartwheel just behind him made him jump – his nerves, he guessed, were still on edge after his experience in the Clink. A bare foot – stiff and grey – protruded from the rear of the cart. It had to be carrying yet more victims to the plague pits. Tom had seen too many such sights in recent days.

Chapter 10

The Anchor

The Anchor had oak beams and a sawdust floor. A few patrons sat around tables wreathed in pipe smoke and drinking from goblets of wine. Tom was heading towards an empty table in the shadow of a large pillar when he heard his name being called. A large, red-faced man with a bushy beard was hailing him from the far side of the room. The man was seated at a table by a bay window overlooking the river. Tom recognized him as Gus Phillips of the King's Men. With him was another man, the playwright Will Shakespeare, whose goblet was at that moment being refilled by a boy.

'Good morrow, Tom,' trumpeted Gus when Tom reached them. 'I've heard you and Adam are doing secret work for the Beagle.'

Tom glanced nervously about, fearful that Watson's spies might be listening in.

'Aye, Mr Phillips,' he replied in a low voice.

'Methinks I would make an excellent spy,' boomed Gus.

'With a voice like yours?' scoffed Will Shakespeare. 'Within hours, the nation's secrets would be known to everyone from Bankside to London Bridge.'

At this the wine boy spoke up: 'But Mr Shakespeare, are not you players a little like spies in the way you take on the guise of another character?'

'A fair point, George,' said Will. 'But it does not apply to Gus, for he is always Gus, whichever role he plays.'

The boy laughed at this, but Gus failed to see the joke. 'Tush, sir, you do disservice to my talents,' he grumbled.

'Nay, it is you who do disservice to my words each time you step on stage,' Will hit back.

Gus sighed. 'You see, Tom, what abuse I must put up with? I am actually a very fine player as anyone around here will tell you. But if Will Shakespeare expects perfection, perhaps he should try writing shorter speeches using less difficult words.'

'Burbage never complains,' muttered Will.

Gus chose to ignore this, turning instead to Tom: 'Tell me, sirrah, what news of Adam? When will he be free to come back to us?'

'I'm hoping later today, Mr Phillips.'

'I too, for tomorrow we are departing on a tour of the provinces.'

'A tour, sir?'

'Aye! The plague has struck London, and all the playhouses have been closed by order of the king. So we must take our show on the road. We'll be performing in Oxford, Barnstaple, Plymouth, Exeter and Dartmouth.'

'*And* Stratford-upon-Avon,' added Shakespeare.

'Marry, sir, I do *not* remember agreeing to include that little backwater on our route,' said Gus.

'Forgive me Mr Phillips,' said young George, 'but you did, while sitting at this very table yesterday afternoon. I had just served you your fourth goblet of wine.'

'Gramercy George,' smiled Will.

'You are paid to bring us drink, sirrah, not listen in on our conversations,' Gus chided the boy. 'Now get back to the kitchen where you belong.'

As George scurried away, Gus sighed and drank some more. 'It's a huge detour to Stratford, Will,' he said. 'It'll mean a lot of extra costs – nights spent in coaching houses, fodder for the horses, food for the players – and all to allow you a brief, sentimental reunion with your family. Why is it so important to you?'

'Because I so rarely get to see them these days,' said Will. 'Do you never get the urge to revisit the tribe of goatherders who begot you?'

'My family are not goatherders,' sniffed Gus. 'But Stratford, Will! Does it even have a decent space for us to perform?'

'Indeed, it has several very fine inn-yards,' said Will. 'The people of Stratford adore the theatre.'

'I'm sure they do,' said Gus glumly. 'I'll vouch we get an audience of fifty yokels who'll understand not a word of what we say, and they'll try and pay us in wool.'

Then his eye lit on something and he brightened. 'Adam!' he cried.

Tom turned in surprise. Alice was making her way across the room towards them. He braced himself for the chill blast of her anger or, worse, her disdain. Instead, to his surprise, she came up and embraced him. It was very brief but fierce, and Tom was left dazed and bewildered by it. After releasing him, she turned to Gus and Will. 'Forgive me, I must speak with Tom a moment in private.'

'Of course,' smirked Gus. 'But don't tarry with him too long, for we must be up with the lark tomorrow. We are embarking on a tour.'

Alice's eyebrows rose. 'A tour? But I... I've never been out of London in my life.'

'Then prepare yourself, my boy, for a scenic expedition through England's green and pleasant pastures, its hills and dales and babbling brooks.' Gus took another swig of wine as his expression soured. 'Its filthy lanes and smelly peasants and foul bogs and flea-bitten townsfolk who wouldn't know culture if it came up and bit them on the behind... Ugh! Will, please remind me why we're doing this?'

'I will see you anon, gentlemen,' said Alice hurriedly,

and she beckoned Tom to follow her. The pair left the tavern, and she led him to a secluded stretch of the river bank behind it.

'You must hate me, Tom,' she said after making sure they were alone.

'What do you mean?' he cried. 'I thought *you* hated *me!*'

'Why would I hate you?'

'For telling Father Watson you might be a spy.'

'But you had no choice!' she said. 'It was all you could do after I nearly ruined everything. And it was absolutely vital you got hold of that message.'

Tom felt gratified beyond measure that she saw things this way. 'How did you nearly ruin everything?' he asked.

'By not knowing the Latin prayers,' said Alice. 'By asking Father Watson if he had ever thought about rebellion. I blundered, Tom, and could easily have got us both killed. But you saved the day, *and* got him to give you the message. I'm so grateful to you.'

Tom was knocked back by these words. Blushing a little, he said: 'When you didn't look at me, I... I thought you were angry.'

'I couldn't look at you, could I?' she said. 'Of course I wanted to, but I had to make him believe we barely knew each other, so that he'd keep trusting you.'

'Aye, that makes sense,' said Tom. 'So what happened after I left? Did he hurt you?'

She shook her head. 'If looks could kill, I'd be a very dead girl by now, but he could do no more than fire his mean stares at me, what with old Kendrick keeping watch on our cell.' She smiled. 'Did *you* arrange that, Tom?'

Tom studied his feet. 'I may have…' he murmured.

She leaned forward and kissed him on the cheek. 'Thank you,' she said.

Tom shivered a little, and his blush deepened. 'It's cold here, by the river,' he lied.

'How's your arm?' she asked. 'I saw him cut you.'

'It's nothing,' said Tom, feeling oddly ashamed of the scar.

'Let me look at it,' she said. 'I've helped our sawbones treat many a player for injuries at the Globe.'

She tried to pull up his sleeve, but Tom tugged his arm free of her grasp. 'Let me alone!' he snapped, and he was surprised at the tears brimming from his eyes.

Alice stepped back, looking somewhat affronted by his attitude. 'Beg pardon,' she muttered.

Tom wiped his eyes and cradled his arm defensively. He'd been branded by that priest like a prize pig – something he didn't wish Alice to know about.

'Well at least will you show me the message he gave you?' she said, and it pained him how she wouldn't meet his eyes.

Tom fumbled for the rolled-up strip in his pocket and handed it to her.

'What sort of weird message is this?' Alice wondered as she carefully unfurled the narrow roll.

Tom edged closer to her, so he could look, too. A column of letters had been written in ink on the inside of the roll.

The letters, read vertically from the top, made no sense.

'P-N-E-T-A-A-E-R...' read Alice, and she wrinkled her nose.

'It must be in code,' said Tom. 'We'll have to crack it before I pass it on to his accomplice.'

'Do you think it might be carriage tracks again, like the last one?'

'I doubt they'd use the same code twice,' said Tom, taking it back from her. 'I'll show it to Sir Francis. He might have some ideas.'

'Who is this accomplice you must take it to?' asked Alice.

'Someone called Sir Griffin Markham. He lives at Bradenstoke Hall in the Forest of Arden.'

Alice bit her lip. 'I wish I was going with you.'

Tom did, too, more than she could know. But he also knew it was impossible. 'We can't be seen together by any of them,' he said. 'Watson thinks you're a spy.'

'I know,' said Alice sadly. 'Besides, I'm expected on this tour.' She attempted a smile. 'Speaking of which, I'd best get back to my friends before Gus gets too drunk. We'll need him sober by the morning or we may end up heading for Dover instead of Dartmouth.' Hesitantly, she took Tom's hand. 'Take care, won't you?'

He opened his mouth to reply, but before he could do so she lifted her head and kissed him again, then turned away. Tom's hand rose to his cheek where her lips had touched his skin. He watched her scurry down some steps and re-enter the tavern.

On his return to York House, Tom was surprised to discover Lord Cecil there. The diminutive spymaster was being entertained by Sir Francis in his library. The two men were seated near the hearth while Owen Jennings, the groom, poured them each a hot drink. Cecil peered doubtfully at the cup handed to him, which contained what looked like steaming reddish-brown water.

'Will it kill me, Francis?' he asked.

'I sincerely hope not,' replied his host, after taking a sip from his own cup. 'The Chinese have been drinking it for centuries, so I'm told, with no ill effect. A Dutch merchant friend of mine, just back from the East, brought me a batch.'

'Does it have a name?'

'They call it *tee*.'

Cecil let a few drops trickle between his lips. 'Hmm,' he frowned. 'The Chinese may like the stuff, but I doubt it'll catch on here.'

Tom cleared his throat to announce his arrival.

'Ah, welcome back Tom,' said Sir Francis. 'Sir Robert has been waiting impatiently for your return.'

'Poley reported that the gaoler released you hours ago,' Cecil said to Tom. 'What took you so long?'

'I was waiting for him to release Adam as well, sire,' Tom replied.

Cecil glowered at him. 'How very *loyal* of you! However, in future, please remember that your first loyalty should be to your country, not your friends.'

He put down his cup. 'Now, what have you got for me? Did Father Watson drop any hints about this plot?'

'He gave me a message,' said Tom.

Cecil's eyes brightened, like a hawk on first sighting its prey. 'A message?'

'Aye, he wants me to deliver it – to someone called Sir Griffin Markham.'

'Sir Griffin Markham,' mused Sir Francis. 'Wasn't he…?'

'A recusant,' said Cecil excitedly, '– living somewhere in Warwickshire, if I'm not mistaken.'

'At Bradenstoke Hall,' said Tom.

'Aye, that's the place,' nodded Cecil. 'We've had our eye on Markham since the Essex Rebellion.' His lips spread in a thin smile. 'This is *excellent* work, Tom Cavendish. You have amply rewarded my faith in you. I expected a few meagre clues. You have given me much much more than that. Will you see the mission through and deliver the message?'

It was posed as a question, but Tom knew by now that Cecil only ever gave orders.

'Aye, my lord.'

'Excellent, because it is vital that you maintain Watson's trust. We want him to believe you are now his loyal minion. At the same time, you must keep your eyes and ears wide open while you're at Bradenstoke Hall. It's quite possible that Lady Arbella herself is being held there. So do please take care to notice and remember everything.

The smallest clue could prove invaluable.'

'I understand, sire.'

'Good! Now let me see the message.'

Tom handed him the roll of paper. 'It's in code.'

'Of course it is,' said Cecil, unwinding it. 'Luckily, we are in the presence of a master codebreaker. What do you make of this, Francis?'

The philosopher rose from his chair and joined Cecil on the far side of the hearth. Together, they scrutinized the nonsensical string of letters.

'The clue,' said Sir Francis after a few moments of silent rumination, 'lies in the form.'

'What do you mean by that?' enquired Cecil.

'These letters could just as easily have been laid out horizontally, could they not? Indeed, that would have made more sense, since people tend to read from left to right. Yet they have been written in a column, to be read, we assume, from top to bottom. So we have to ask ourselves why would Watson do that?'

'And?' coaxed Cecil. 'Why *would* he do it?'

'There is only one reason I can think of,' said Sir Francis. 'It appears to me that Watson has employed the Spartan scytale.'

'The Spartan what?'

'The Spartan scytale is, to my knowledge, the only coding method that requires messages to be written out in this form.'

Sir Francis began pacing the floor, raising his finger as he spoke, in the manner of a university lecturer.

'The Spartan scytale is a very ancient type of code,' he said. 'Indeed, it dates back to the time of the Spartans, who were, as I'm sure you are aware, obsessed with fighting and warfare. And it turns out that the scytale is an ideal method of encoding battlefield communications...'

'Enough, Francis!' interjected Cecil. 'This is not the time for a history lesson. Just tell us how we can break it.'

Sir Francis stopped in mid-step, mouth open, finger pointing ceilingwards. Then he offered a sheepish smile. 'That's the tricky part,' he confessed. 'You see, the scytale is actually a wooden staff around which a strip of paper containing coded letters can be wound. If the staff is of the correct thickness, then the letters on the strip will align to form the message. The receiver, Sir Griffin, will know exactly how thick the staff should be. The trouble is, we don't.'

'Well can we not try various staffs until we find one that works?' asked Cecil.

'We could,' said Sir Francis, 'though that may take some time...'

'We don't have that luxury,' said Cecil. 'The conspirators are plotting the downfall of this kingdom as we speak. What's more, if Tom doesn't deliver the message promptly, Watson and Markham may grow suspicious.'

'In that case, let me make a copy,' said Sir Francis, rummaging in his desk for a writing implement and a spare scrap of parchment. 'Tom can deliver the original while I get to work on cracking the code.'

'Agreed,' said Cecil, rising from his chair.

'More *tee* before you go, sire?' Owen offered the chief minister.

Cecil scowled at him and swept from the room.

Act Three

Chapter 11

Gentlemen of the Road

THE ROAD TO BRADENSTOKE HALL,

5TH MAY 1603

Tom departed York House for Bradenstoke Hall early the next morning. Sir Francis had furnished him with a black Neapolitan courser named Gunpowder. It wasn't the youngest or fastest horse in his stable. (As Sir Francis put it, 'We don't want Markham thinking you can afford to hire top-quality transportation.') But Tom soon found it made up for these deficiencies with stamina and a fine temperament.

Tom had been taught to ride by his uncle, and had accompanied his former master the Earl of Essex on numerous hunting trips in Greenwich Park, so he was comfortable in the saddle. Yet until now, he hadn't ventured more than ten miles from the capital. The journey to Bradenstoke was at least ten times that distance, on unfamiliar roads, with only the odd signpost or passerby to guide him.

On his first night, he stayed at an inn near Oxford. He arrived after sunset, sweat-streaked and filthy from the road, to find all the rooms had been taken, which meant he was obliged to spend the night on a mound of smelly straw above the stable, fighting off the mice that kept scurrying across his face and body. The following evening, after another arduous day's ride, he reached the city of Warwick, where he encountered an establishment called the Roebuck and a much friendlier reception. In the cobbled yard, the ostler unsaddled Gunpowder and led him through to the stables, then carried Tom's saddle bag into the inn. The friendly innkeeper showed Tom to his chamber. Tom was delighted to find a room with glazed windows, a bed with posts and curtains around it, clean linen sheets and feather-filled pillows. A bowl of dried fragrant flowers had been placed on the table to sweeten the air, a ewer of water and a basin was provided for washing, and there was even a chamberpot beneath the bed. This was luxury beyond anything he was accustomed to. But Cecil had provided him with ample funds to cover his expenses, so he was not worried about the bill.

That evening, Tom dined with his fellow guests on tasty pottage and salted beef while a musician played the lute and sang for them. Life on the road, he decided, was not so bad after all. When supper was over, he was provided with a candle to see his way to bed. Thoroughly exhausted after two days of hard travel, he slept more soundly than he had for many a night. The following morning, an hour or so after dawn, he settled his bill and summoned the stableboy. Gunpowder was fetched from the stable, looking similarly well rested and fed. Tom then galloped into the Forest of Arden for the final ten miles of his journey to Bradenstoke Hall.

Unknown to him, the ostler who had very kindly relieved him of his saddle bag in the innyard the night before, had then taken the liberty of examining its contents. Later that evening, for the price of a drink, the ostler had informed a couple of smartly dressed guests at the inn that Tom was in possession of a goodly sum of money. The guests had risen earlier than Tom, dressed themselves in their fancy attire (the spoils of a previous robbery), and were now laying in wait for him in the forest.

Tom rode innocently into their trap. On a narrow path lined on both sides with dense trees, he was forced to a halt as a horse rider suddenly erupted out of the forest ten yards ahead of him. When the man raised his pistol, Tom tried desperately to turn Gunpowder about, only to discover a second pistol-wielding fellow blocking the path behind.

'Fear not, my young friend,' shouted the first robber. 'We desire only your money. Prithee, get down from your horse, throw your bag onto the road and raise your hands so we can see them.'

Tremblingly, Tom did as he was told. The men then also dismounted and approached him. One of them made straight for the saddle bag and began emptying it onto the ground. Tom watched in consternation as his spare clothing, his pewter bowl and cup and, most alarmingly, Watson's rolled-up message, all went tumbling onto the muddy track. The robber then proceeded to stuff all these items into his own canvas bag, including the message.

'Wait!' said his companion, who was looking not at the saddle bag or its contents but at Tom. The highwayman appeared to be studying Tom's right arm, which had been partially exposed by the action of raising his hands above his head. Suddenly, the highwayman's eyes widened, his face paled and his body became extremely rigid.

The other one, meanwhile, was on his haunches, hefting the purse in his hand. 'Zounds! We have a fat one here,' he chuckled. 'Enough I'll wager for a few more nights at the Roebuck.'

'Give it back,' murmured his friend.

'Eh? What's that?' The man looked up, puzzled.

'Put it back in the young man's bag, Jack, along with everything else you took. And be quick about it.'

The robber spoke these words through very dry

lips, while standing stock still, his eyes never leaving Tom's arm.

The other man now caught sight of what his partner was looking at, and he began to shiver. 'Oh my!' he blubbered. 'Oh heavens! Pray forgive us, sir! We weren't to know!' He dropped the purse as if it was made of fire, then on his knees he crawled over to Tom and prostrated himself before him. 'We humbly beseech you, sir, show us mercy and by my troth we'll leave this forest this very day and you'll never see or hear of us again.'

Tom was too surprised to speak. He could only watch, astonished, as the man, with frantic haste, replaced all his possessions in his saddle bag, which was then laid carefully, like a sacrificial offering, at his feet. After a few more grovelling apologies, the bandits hastily remounted their chargers and galloped away down the track. It was only when they were out of sight that Tom realised he still had his hands raised in the air. He lowered them and looked at his right arm with its 'fish' scar.

How could such a little thing inspire so much fear?

Of course, he was relieved that the robbers had fled without taking his possessions. But he also felt unsettled by their reaction to the scar, and what it signified about the circle of people he had unwillingly joined.

Chapter 12

The Face at the Window

BRADENSTOKE HALL, 5TH MAY 1603

One hour later, Tom trotted up to the gates of Bradenstoke Hall. A grey stone wall surrounded the property, above which could be seen the battlements on the gatehouse.

Stay calm, he told himself as a burly man emerged from the guardhouse carrying a long, cruel-looking halberd.

Remember, you're a recusant, a former cell mate of Father Watson.

'State your business,' said the guard, who had a red birthmark covering most of his face.

'I've come up from London with an urgent message for Sir Griffin Markham.'

'Dismount,' ordered the guard.

Tom did so, then stood passively as the guard slowly and methodically searched his person and his saddle bag – for hidden weapons, he presumed.

At length, the guard gave a whistle and a boy of about ten came out of the guardhouse and unlocked the gate. The boy was small and lithe with a pale face and long black shaggy locks.

'Roland, escort this young man to Sir Griffin,' the guard told him.

'Follow me,' Roland said to Tom. Moving with a confident swagger, the boy took Gunpowder by the reins and began leading him over a stone bridge towards the gatehouse. Tom, tagging along behind, stared at the green, sun-dappled surface of the moat. A mother duck was leading her young brood near some reeds. The day was already warm, and Tom felt a curious urge to throw off all his clothes and dive in.

They were nearing the end of the bridge and entering the shadow of the gatehouse when Tom heard a distant, echoing splash. He looked up to his left in time to see a circle of spreading ripples in the moat, close to the mossy base of the house's main wall. Did someone throw something out of the window? He couldn't see anyone there. But lifting his gaze to the second-storey window, he glimpsed a face. Almost before he had become fully conscious of it, it vanished from sight.

'Hurry up!' said Roland, waiting impatiently for him at the far end of the bridge. Tom followed the lad through the vaulted passage beneath the gatehouse and out into the sunlit courtyard beyond. He took in the ivy-clad walls and, above them, the pretty, half-timbered gables. It was not exactly how he had imagined a hideout for a bunch of dangerous fanatics.

Notice and remember everything! Cecil had urged him. Tom scanned the dark, mullioned windows overlooking the courtyard. Could Lady Arbella be imprisoned behind one of those? … Or might she have been that person he'd glimpsed at the window above the moat? The face had disappeared before he could ascertain if it was a man or a woman. Perhaps if it was she, her plan had been to try and attract his attention by tossing something into the moat, but then she'd had to step out of sight before the boy or the guard at the gate saw her. Tom wondered if he should try and communicate with her while he was here – reassure her that help was on the way. But to do that risked blowing his cover. Cecil had asked him to check for clues, not try and speak to the prisoner.

Once Gunpowder had been stabled, Roland ushered Tom into the house. In the great hall, the boy stopped and cocked his head. Drifting in from one of the adjoining rooms was the sound of a raised voice…

'Take care with them, sirrah! If you drop them I'll make you go out and kill me another animal!'

'He's in the drawing room,' said Roland, swaggering across the hall and opening one of the doors. Tom entered behind him.

A sturdily built man was standing in the middle of a small room watching a servant on a ladder trying to fix an enormous pair of stag's antlers – the trophy, Tom guessed, of a recent hunt – on the oak-panelled wall. 'They're not straight, Hastings,' said the watching man. 'Make 'em straighter.'

The servant had a mouthful of nails and a hammer in the crook of his elbow. He wobbled on the ladder as he tried to adjust the angle of the wooden plaque on which the antlers had been mounted.

'Sir Griffin,' said Roland. 'Forgive the intrusion, sir, but this man has a message for you. He's just rode up from London.'

Markham spun around to face Tom. He had pink cheeks, a full beard and straggly black hair that hung well below the collar of his doublet.

'A message?' he said. 'From whom?'

'Father Watson,' answered Tom.

Markham's grey eyes became very still. 'Father Watson, eh? And who is Father Watson?'

A trickle of sweat started to slide down the back of Tom's neck. 'He's a–a priest, sir. He claims to know you.'

'Does he now?' Markham examined Tom very carefully as if he were a work of intricate craftsmanship that might just cut off his finger if he tried to handle it. 'Well I don't know any Father Watson. So why don't you take yourself back to your masters, sirrah, before I convey you to the highest window in my house and toss you into the moat.'

Tom stared at him, stupefied.

'I pay my fines for not attending church,' blustered Markham, his cheeks growing even rosier. 'I've sworn an oath of loyalty to the king. What more do you people want of me? Tell your masters if they are trying to entrap me, they're wasting their time. I'm done with plots and conspiracies. My days of rebellion are over. I'm just an innocent man doing his best to live his life in...'

Markham's mouth and voice stopped working just then as Tom rolled up his sleeve. While Markham was staring at the exposed fish scar, there came a resounding crash from behind him: the ladder had collapsed and servant and antlers went tumbling. The servant groaned, the antlers cracked. But Markham didn't blink. His eyes remained fixed on the scar. Then he pushed up the sleeve of his doublet and showed, etched on his pale forearm, the same sign. Tom nodded solemnly, trying his best to act like a member of a secret circle acknowledging his fellow.

'Forgive me, friend,' Markham said after a moment. 'You understand how careful I must be... Prithee, hand over the message.'

Tom rummaged in his bag and pulled out the roll of paper. Markham snatched it from him and eagerly uncoiled it. He pored over the seemingly random chain of letters like a scholar studying an ancient manuscript.

'Leave me, Roland!' he barked at the boy, who was still hovering near the door. Roland backed out of the room. 'You, too, Hastings!' Markham said to the fallen servant. Rubbing his aching hip, the servant limped from the room.

Tom hoped Markham might allow him, as a fellow member of the 'brotherhood of the fish', to remain. That way, he'd be able to discover the meaning of the message, and see for himself how to crack the code.

But it was not to be.

'I pray pardon, friend,' said Markham. 'This message, and the means of interpreting it, are too secret to be revealed, even to your good self. Now if you would be so good as to step outside, Roland will take you to the kitchen for some refreshment. I will call for you when I am ready with my own message, also coded, in response to this one.'

Suppressing a grimace of disappointment, Tom bowed and left the room, almost tripping over a broken antler as he did so. The hallway outside was empty – neither Roland nor Hastings were anywhere to be seen. On the far side of the hall, through a shadowy archway, rose a set of steps. This, Tom suddenly realised, was his chance. While no one was around, and Markham was preoccupied, he could steal upstairs and try and speak with Lady Arbella. If he was seen at any stage by a servant, he could always claim to have got lost on his way to find Roland.

Tom swiftly crossed the hall, passed beneath the arch and mounted the staircase. At the top he found a wide, sunlit corridor overlooking the courtyard. From the window, he could see the towering gatehouse to his right. Using this to orient himself, he calculated the location of the room where he'd seen the figure. It ought to be just around the corner from where he was standing. Tom walked quickly along the corridor, taking care to keep to the gloomier side, away from the windows. He followed it as it bent sharply to the left, and then stopped at the first door he came to after the corner. Next to the door was a stool and, leaning up against the wall, a sword. A guard had been here, and might be back very soon, most probably after a visit to the jakes. So a prisoner was being kept here. He shuddered to think that Lady Arbella might be on the other side of this very door. After checking that he was quite alone, Tom approached the door and knocked quietly yet firmly.

There was no response.

Slowly, he turned the handle and tried to open the door. It was locked.

He leaned down and placed his mouth close to the keyhole beneath the handle. 'Lady Arbella,' he whispered hoarsely. 'Are you there?'

From within the room, Tom began to hear sounds: the creak of a bed, the soft pad of footsteps. *She was coming.*

Then a tired, weak, decidedly male voice said: 'I am Richard. Are you the one I saw just now crossing the moat?'

'Aye,' said Tom, disappointed.

'I'm being held prisoner by Sir Griffin Markham,' said Richard. 'You must help me escape.'

Tom sighed. He hadn't anticipated finding *another* prisoner. This made everything much more complicated.

'The door's locked,' he said.

'There's only one guard,' said Richard, who had evidently thought through the problem. 'I heard him put his sword down before he left. When he comes back, use the sword to force him to open the door with his key. I'll take care of everything after that.'

'You'll take care of everything,' Tom repeated numbly. He stared at the sword, and swallowed.

'You won't be caught,' hissed Richard. 'I will get us both out of here. I know the house. I know how to escape... Now, quickly. Pick up the sword and hide somewhere close by, ready to jump out at the guard. The suit of armour by the window opposite will do as a hiding-place.'

Tom glanced at the suit of armour behind him. It was small – probably too small to conceal him.

'Hurry!' pleaded Richard. 'He'll be back at any moment.'

Tom recalled Cecil's words: *It's vital that you maintain Watson's trust.*

Sometimes, sacrifices needed to be made.

He bent closer to the keyhole. 'I can't,' he said. 'Please forgive me.'

He felt sorry for the young man. But if he helped him escape, Markham would realise he was a government spy. The mission would be over. The conspirators would be alerted to Cecil's activities and they would quickly vanish from sight, along with Lady Arbella.

'Please!' breathed Richard.

'Forgive me,' Tom said. 'I cannot help you…' He squirmed, knowing how callous he was about to sound. 'Richard, I'm looking for a woman, Lady Arbella Stuart. Is she here at Bradenstoke Hall?'

Richard went quiet. Tom waited desperately for him to reply. He glanced up and down the corridor. It was still empty.

'Aye, she's here,' said Richard finally. 'If you let me out, I'll lead you to her.'

Tom's pulse quickened. *Could it be true? Had he just managed to find the most sought-after woman in the kingdom?* But then he began to have doubts – was this just a ruse by Richard to persuade Tom to help him escape from the room? How could this young man know anything, trapped in here?

Suddenly, Tom heard footsteps approaching from around the corner. He glanced once more at the sword. Then, with a sigh, he hastened away in the opposite direction. He barged into the room above the gatehouse. To his right he spotted an arched entrance leading to another room overlooking the moat. Boots squeaked on the floorboards outside. Someone was about to enter. Tom flew through the archway into the adjoining room, which was filled with winches and chains connected to a huge, heavy iron lattice – the portcullis. At one end of the room was a set of descending spiral steps. Tom almost fell down these before tumbling through a narrow door into the vaulted passageway beneath the gatehouse. He picked himself up and began sprinting across the courtyard.

'You! I've been looking for you!' squeaked a small figure standing at the entrance to the great hall. It was Roland. 'Where did you get to?'

'I–I was looking for *you*,' said Tom, skidding to a breathless halt.

Roland handed Tom his saddlebag. 'Here, you left this in the drawing room. I put the message in there – the one Sir Griffin wants you to pass on to Father Watson. You'll also find some bread and cheese, and a few coins for your trouble.'

'Thank you,' said Tom.

'Now wait here while I fetch your horse,' said the boy. 'Don't run away again.'

Chapter 13

It Droppeth as the Gentle Rain...

STRATFORD-UPON-AVON, 7ᵀᴴ MAY 1603

The convoy of four wagons came trundling towards Stratford-upon-Avon, their canvas canopies fluttering like ship sails in a high breeze. They approached from the east through a wide green meadow of grazing cows. The River Avon flowed in a lazy curve around this side of the town, spanned by an elegant stone bridge with fourteen arches. As the convoy reached the far side of the bridge, Alice Fletcher peered out of the leading wagon in great excitement.

'So this is your home town, Mr Shakespeare,' she said. 'Are you delighted to be back?'

Will, seated on the bench beside her, smiled. 'Each time I return, I am reminded quite forcefully of the reason why I left. Stratford is a small place, not so much in size but in spirit. Yet I am looking forward to seeing my family again.'

As they jolted along the muddy street, they passed thatched cottages and then some larger timber-framed houses.

'There's my old school,' said Will, pointing to a long, low building with whitewashed timbers and wooden struts across the windows. 'I was studying there when a theatrical troupe came to town – the first I'd ever seen. I couldn't have been more than ten. I remember being enthralled by the performance of the clown, Richard Tarlton. That speech I gave Hamlet about Yorick – the fellow of infinite jest – that was my tribute to Tarlton... I wanted to run away with those players. They showed me a glimpse of another kind of life. But I was too young...'

Gus Phillips shuffled over to them from the front of the wagon. 'I confess this is not quite the backwater I had anticipated, Will. It is a substantial town.'

'I'm glad you think so,' replied Will.

'I hope we might be permitted to perform at the Guild Hall. It looks like a wonderful space. Could you perhaps pull some strings with the council? Was your father not the local alderman or something while he was alive?'

'My father was a great many things while he was

alive,' answered Will, 'but now he isn't, and any strings there might have been were severed with his death.'

'I struggle to believe that,' said Gus. 'You told me once you'd bought the second biggest house in Stratford, by which I assumed you meant a hovel with two rooms rather than the usual one. But on this evidence I see you must have purchased a sizeable property. I'll vouch you have some stature in this town, Will. You're a big fish in a small pond...'

'A fish of whatever size who abandons his pond for a larger one is rarely welcomed back,' remarked the playwright.

'Is that your house, Mr Shakespeare?' asked Alice, pointing to an impressive property coming up on the right.

'Aye, that's the hovel,' said Will.

The house, known as New Place, had expensive brick instead of plasterwork between its timber frames, a wide central porch, and five windows on each of its top two floors. The top-floor windows were set within tall, imposing gables.

'It's beautiful,' gasped Alice.

'Why don't we stop here for some luncheon?' suggested Will. 'My wife keeps a well-stocked pantry.'

'An excellent plan!' said Gus, and he went to alert the driver.

The wagons pulled up on Chapel Lane, which ran along the side of the house, and the players eagerly leapt out to stretch their legs. Such was the volume of their excited chatter, they soon attracted the attention of people nearby, including the residents of New Place. An upper-floor window was flung open, out of which floated a peal of feminine laughter, and a moment later two young women ran out into the street.

'Susannah! Judith!' exclaimed Will, as he embraced them.

'Oh, Father! Father!' they responded, laughing and crying at the same time.

Alice stood by and watched the family reunite: the daughters, flush-cheeked and shiny-eyed, relating their news as Will gazed at them with fatherly pride and affection. Alice was happy for Will. Yet she couldn't help a thickness forming in her throat and a hollow sort of pain in her chest. Witnessing his joy was a stark reminder of her own irreparable loss.

Soon, two older women emerged from the house – Will's wife, Anne, and his mother, Mary. Alice noticed a stiffness and formality about the way he greeted Anne. But when he embraced Mary, the sentiment seemed more genuine, and his eyes glittered with filial love and tears. She looked frail, and Alice suspected she'd visibly aged since Will had last laid eyes on her – perhaps the toll of losing her husband. There seemed to be some measure of guilt in his expression – he had not been here for her.

Will introduced the player-sharers to his family – Gus Phillips, Richard Burbage, John Heminges, Robert Armin and Henry Condell. Next, he introduced the three hired men and three prentices who had joined them on the tour. The first of the prentices to be presented was Alice, who Will referred to as 'my dear, talented friend, Adam', bringing a blush to her cheeks.

After Will explained that he would like to offer his fellow players some sustenance, Anne sent her daughters to market with a long list of things to buy, including 'a quarter of mutton, some pickled conger eel, a stubble goose, eggs, figs, coleworts, lettuce, sage, garlic, rampions, chervil and onions'.

'Your wife certainly knows how to entertain, Will,' said Gus, openly salivating.

During luncheon, Alice found herself seated next to Judith, the younger of Will's daughters. She had her grandmother's round face framed by dark ringlets, her father's lively eyes and a small, red mouth that was in constant motion, for the young lady seemed to love both eating and talking. Between mouthfuls, she confided to Alice a particular item of family gossip.

'My sister,' said Judith, 'is in love with a dashing and highly eligible young man named John Hall. He's a physician, you know. Indeed, he's the only physician in Stratford, so you can imagine how busy he is. And he's a Puritan, too, and always going to church. Susannah is completely in love with him.'

Alice glanced at Susannah, who was fortunately seated out of earshot at the far end of the table. Not as conventionally pretty as Judith, she had a squarish jaw and a somewhat large nose. Yet Alice thought she had a very pleasant face – especially when she smiled, which she was managing to do, quite heroically, in the company of Gus Phillips.

'I believe Mr Hall is planning to propose to Susannah one of these days,' said Judith, 'though he's so busy with his patients, I'm sure he hardly has time to put his mind to such trifles as marriage proposals. Susannah says he studied medicine in France. He's so very sophisticated. And quite devout. Did I tell you he's a Puritan? I shall be most fortunate to have him as a brother-in-law, should he ever find the time to propose.'

'And you, Judith?' Alice asked. 'Are you in love with anyone?'

'I?' giggled Judith. 'Oh no!' She blushed, and glanced at Richard Burbage who was seated opposite, pipe in hand, conversing with Robert Armin. 'I could imagine myself falling for a player, though. Some of them seem quite… dashing.'

'I wouldn't waste your time with that one,' said Alice. 'Half the women in London are in love with Mr Burbage – including the queen of England, when she was alive.'

'In faith! Is that so?' giggled Judith.

'He turns your father's poetry into sweet music for the masses,' said Alice. 'He can melt a heart at a hundred paces. You should have seen his Hamlet two years ago.'

'I would that I had,' breathed Judith.

'You will see his Shylock tonight in our play,

The Merchant of Venice. That will be a treat for you.'

'Truly, I cannot wait…' Judith stuffed some mutton into her mouth and chewed upon it a little despondently. 'Alas, there are no players here in Stratford to speak of. I shall most probably have to settle for marrying a tradesman – a glover or a vintner. There are plenty of those sorts around here.'

'There's nothing wrong with tradesmen,' murmured Alice. 'Or servants for that matter…'

Her mind faded for a moment, and she was back by the Thames, behind the Anchor tavern. She had very nearly cried when she'd said goodbye to Tom – and was relieved she hadn't done so in front of him. He'd become important to her – she had to acknowledge this fact, however unwelcome it was. Losing her brother Richard had torn her in two. She had never recovered, and never would. Since then, she'd tried very hard to protect herself from further damage by refusing to allow anyone to get too close to her. She had built a wall of rock around her heart – that was how she imagined it anyway. But somehow, Tom had breached it. When and how had this happened? Was it last week, when she watched him deal with the monstrous priest, Father Watson, in the Clink? Or was it last year, when he came to see her perform as Viola in *Twelfth Night*, and afterwards she'd wept about Richard and he'd comforted her? Maybe she was fooling herself. Was it possible he'd broken through her heart's wall the very day she first laid eyes on him, beneath the stage during that performance of *Hamlet*? Perhaps she'd just spent the past two years denying the truth.

'Are you alright, Adam?' asked Judith.

Alice shook herself out of her reverie.

'Aye, forgive me,' she said. 'I was dreaming.'

'About a maid?'

'Pardon?'

'You were, weren't you?' giggled Judith. 'You were dreaming about a maid.'

'Aye,' said Alice. 'Aye, that was it. A maid. She went on a journey, and now I fear for her safety. I wish... I wish I could have gone with her, to protect her...'

'Where did she go?'

'Hm?'

'Your sweetheart?'

'Oh, she went... She went...'

It suddenly occurred to Alice that Tom had gone to a place in Warwickshire, where they were now – perhaps he wasn't so far away after all. Yet he'd left a week ago, and was almost certainly back in London by now. Wherever he was, she prayed he was safe.

The sky had darkened while they were eating, and now a loud crack of thunder made everyone turn their heads to the window.

'It's lucky we won't be performing in the local innyard this evening,' smiled Gus, as heavy raindrops began spattering the glass.

'Speaking of which, isn't it high time we confirmed the Guild Hall as this evening's venue?' said John

Heminges. 'You should go to the council offices now.'

'Pray, let me finish my wine first, sir,' said Gus. 'There's no rush. They'll be falling over themselves to offer us the Guild Hall. Towns like this are always eager for a taste of London culture.'

When Gus had finished his wine, he and Will donned their hats and cloaks and made a dash through the storm for the Council Chamber.

Less than an hour later, they were back, their clothes dripping, their moods bitter and depressed. They threw themselves disconsolately into armchairs by the fire as the others gathered to hear the news.

'God's teeth! I hate Puritans,' growled Gus.

'Kill-joys,' muttered Will. 'Desecrators of delight...'

'Father!' said Susannah, horrified.

'What happened?' asked John Heminges.

'The Council has been taken over by a bunch of dour religious fanatics,' said Gus. 'They've banned plays from the Guild Hall and every other public building in Stratford. If we dare try and put on the play here, we risk a steep fine that will wipe out our profits.'

'Can we not find an innyard to host us?' asked Robert Armin.

'Aye, I dare say we can,' said Gus, staring dismally through the window at the rain.

During the course of the afternoon, the rain eased off, and Gus, Will and Alice ventured out into the muddy, puddled streets to scout for possible venues. Most innkeepers were reluctant to defy the Puritan councillors, but they eventually met with success at the Greyhound on the High Street. The toothless widow who ran the establishment gleefully informed them that her inn was famous in these parts because, some years ago, a plague outbreak began here.

'Delightful!' muttered Gus.

Will seemed to derive much amusement from the look on Gus's face. 'Welcome to Stratford,' he smirked.

The innyard at the Greyhound was modest in size, and when the wind blew in the wrong direction, it carried foul smells from the town midden and the tannery.

Still, it was better than nothing.

The players spent the rest of the afternoon distributing their playbills around the town, or helping to set up the stage and the props, trying their best to recreate a romantic vision of Venice in the shabby, malodorous little yard.

At six o'clock, when they were ready to begin their performance, the rain started up again, and a small yet noisy group of local Puritans took up position outside the inn chanting their displeasure. Nevertheless, a small number of the town's residents braved the weather and the threats of eternal damnation to come and watch the play. Altogether, some fifty curious locals gathered in the yard that evening, and only a few of them tried to pay in wool.

Chapter 14

Lutes and Poppy seeds

YORK HOUSE, 8ᵀᴴ MAY 1603

'I think Lady Arbella may be at Bradenstoke Hall,' said Tom.

'You *think* she may be there?' queried Cecil.

They were in Sir Francis Bacon's library at York House. It was mid-morning and Tom had arrived back a short while ago from his journey to Warwickshire. The master of the house was elsewhere, most probably in his study, still trying to crack the code Watson had used for his message. Cecil was standing at the library's large bay window, staring through Sir Francis's 'seeing-tube' – a brass cylinder with lenses at either end, which made distant objects appear closer. Tom, standing over by the hearth, could not make out what Cecil was looking at. Was he trying to see all the way to Warwickshire?

'The young man I met,' said Tom, '– the one who called himself Richard – he said Lady Arbella was there.'

'And do you have any reason to doubt his word?'

'He'd been begging me to let him out of the room. He may have said she was there, and that he would lead me to her, just so I would help him escape.'

'Or he may have been telling the truth.' Cecil lowered the seeing-tube and turned to Tom. His face was in shadow, but Tom could tell his expression was sombre.

'Aye, my lord,' conceded Tom.

'You made a judgement,' said Cecil.

'I had very little time, sire,' said Tom. 'A guard was coming...' He began to explain in more detail the dilemma he had faced in that upper-floor corridor.

'So you had the advantage of surprise,' Cecil concluded. 'You had a sword available to you, and a hiding-place. It would have been the work of a minute to overpower the guard and force him to open the door. If this Richard fellow had been telling the truth, the two of you could have rescued Lady Arbella and escaped, and this crisis we are facing – this grave threat to the realm – could have been resolved.'

Tom's shoulders slumped. 'When you put it like that, sire, I feel I have failed you,' he said.

Cecil's thin mouth crinkled into a smile. 'On the contrary, Tom. You've done very well. Your decision was precisely the one I would have taken had I been in your shoes.'

This reaction both heartened and confused Tom. 'What do you mean, sire?'

'What I mean is that you were wise not to listen to this young man. His suggestion was both reckless and foolhardy. Think of all that could have gone wrong. What if you couldn't overpower the guard? Or what if his cries had alerted others nearby? Even if the rescue had been successful, what if Richard had been lying about Lady Arbella or his ability to escape the house?

'But let's imagine the most optimistic scenario: you prevail over the guard, you free Richard, and you and he then manage to locate and liberate Lady Arbella – even then, you would have faced a formidable challenge trying to escape from such a well-guarded house with its wide moat and high wall.

'This young man may have had nothing to lose, but you had plenty. It was vital to us that you maintained your cover as a loyal supporter of Markham and Watson. That, above all, was the purpose of this mission, and in that you were successful. So I congratulate you in not trying to be the hero. The first rule of spying is to exercise caution and keep a low profile. You managed to do both, and you also gathered some useful intelligence in the process.'

'Thank you, my lord,' said Tom, greatly warmed by these words, though not entirely sure he deserved them. During those moments outside Richard's door, he'd been quite close to panic – hardly the cool, calculating figure of Cecil's description. Yet, now he thought about it, hadn't he been able to think with reasonable clarity, despite the pressure he was under? Perhaps he did have a future as a spy.

'What will you do now, sire?' Tom asked. 'Will you storm Bradenstoke Hall and see if you can find Lady Arbella there?'

'Nay. I prefer to wait a little longer and see how this plot plays out. I sense there are more people involved than just Watson and Markham, and I want to catch them all. We must continue to play the game, Tom. You must deliver the message to Watson in the Clink and, if necessary, carry his reply back to Bradenstoke. I just wish I knew what they were saying to each other. How long can it take to crack a code?'

'Longer than you may think,' said a voice from the doorway.

They both looked up to see Sir Francis striding in, a long strip of paper streaming from his fingertips – his copy of the coded message. His mouth formed a tight line, and his nostrils were flared. It was an expression Tom had seen before, following the failure of an experiment.

'Three days ago, I visited a woodturner's workshop on Cheapside,' Sir Francis said in a somewhat brittle voice. 'I commissioned him to produce a set of cylinders of various diameters, ranging from one to ten inches. I took delivery of them yesterday, and have spent the intervening time attempting to find my scytale. Not one of the cylinders has yielded anything but nonsense. It is most dispiriting.'

'Perhaps Watson used another coding method,' suggested Cecil.

'Nay, sir. He used a scytale, of that I am sure. All I lack is the diameter. But perhaps there is a clue here on the message itself. There was something I noticed while I was transcribing it – well, two things. They may just be doodles, but I copied them down anyway...' Sir Francis gathered up the long band of paper until he had its tail end in his hand. 'Ah, here they are, right at the bottom. What do you make of them?'

Tom and Cecil came closer and peered at a pair of tiny drawings at the very tip of the paper. The drawing on the left consisted of a thick vertical line encircled at the bottom by a pear-shaped oval. Within this oval, and attached to the line, was a second, much thinner line, which curved away from the thick line like a branch splitting off from the trunk of a tree. The drawing on the right was a circle with a vertical line dangling beneath it and what looked like a flower coming out of its top.

'I tried to copy them as precisely as I could,' said Sir Francis. 'I used the seeing-tube to help me study them in detail – just in case they have some meaning.'

'And?' said Cecil.

Sir Francis shook his head. 'They are probably just doodles.'

'This one could be a lute,' said Tom, indicating the

drawing on the left.

'A lute?' murmured Sir Francis, bending to look once more.

'A lute with a broken string,' added Tom.

'A broken string… Do you mean that thin, curving line coming off the vertical line? Aye, I see what you mean.'

'A lute with a broken string,' frowned Cecil. 'What sort of a clue is that?'

Sir Francis began muttering to himself. 'A lute… with a broken string… Now, where have I seen that before?'

Suddenly, his eyes brightened and the reddish whiskers of his beard bristled. 'Why, of course! "The Ambassadors"!' he cried. 'There's a lute with a broken string in "The Ambassadors".'

'You mean the painting by Holbein?' queried Cecil.

Sir Francis nodded vigorously.

Tom remembered the painting all too well – it had hung in the picture gallery at Essex House. He kicked himself for not having made the connection.

'And why is that significant?' asked Cecil.

'*Everything* about that painting is significant, is it not, Tom?'

'Aye, sir,' said Tom, readily agreeing.

'Think about it, Robert,' said Sir Francis. 'Watson and Markham were involved in the Essex Rebellion of two years ago.'

'True,' acknowledged Cecil.

'Which means they were both, for a time at least,

based at Essex House, and in those days, Essex House was home to…

'"The Ambassadors",' finished Cecil.

'Precisely!'

Cecil nodded. 'A fair point, Francis. But where does it take us? How do we get from a painting to a diameter for the scytale? We need a number, do we not?'

'"The Ambassadors" is full of numbers,' said Sir Francis. 'We just have to work out which number they are referring to.'

'Might it be a number pertaining to the lute?' posited Cecil.

Sir Francis frowned and shook his head. 'I doubt it. There aren't any particular numbers associated with the lute. I think it's just there to symbolise the painting…'

'So how many numbers are in the painting altogether?' asked Cecil.

'Dozens,' confessed Sir Francis. 'More than I know of, most probably.'

'So we're not actually any closer to solving this!'

Sir Francis looked decidedly sheepish.

'There is a number that keeps cropping up in that painting,' said Tom. 'It's a number that was certainly known to Sir Gelly Meyrick, because it enabled him to find the priest hole.'

Both men looked up sharply. 'You mean Devereux's steward – one of the ringleaders of the rebellion?' said Cecil. 'Well, if he knew it, then I've no doubt Markham and Watson did, too.'

'What is the number?' asked Sir Francis.

'Twenty-seven, sir. It appears in lots of places in the painting.'

Sir Francis winced. 'That's far too big a number, Tom. A twenty-seven-inch diameter scytale would be as fat as an oak tree. Our strip of paper wouldn't even twist around it once.'

'Maybe they're not talking about inches,' said Cecil.

'What unit of measurement is smaller than an inch?' Sir Francis challenged him.

'Barleycorns?' suggested Cecil. 'Poppy seeds?' Then he yelped in pain – for Sir Francis had suddenly grabbed his arm and was squeezing it with great force.

'What's got into you, Francis?' he spluttered. 'Unhand me at once!'

'Did you just say… *poppy seeds*?'

'Aye, rather an obscure unit that one, not often used,' Cecil grimaced. 'According to the clerks of the market it means one twelfth of an inch. Now *prithee*, let me go!'

At last, Sir Francis released his grip on the chief minister, but only so he could point once more at the strip of paper – this time at the little drawing on the right. 'This,' he said, 'is a poppyseed pod. The line down here is the stalk. The circle with its flower-like crown is the pod. Don't you see? It's telling us we should measure the diameter in poppy seeds.'

Cecil looked doubtful. 'This is all rather speculative,

Francis. We're making a lot of assumptions…'

But Sir Francis wasn't listening. He was muttering calculations under his breath: 'One twelfth of an inch multiplied by twenty-seven? Now, let me see… That would mean a diameter of… two and a quarter inches. By Jove, that could work!'

'Will you need to commission another scytale from your woodturner to test out your farfetched theory?' asked Cecil.

Sir Francis shook his head. 'I should be able to use my two-inch one and wrap cloth around it to a depth of a quarter inch. Tom, can you organise it for me?'

'Aye, sir,' said Tom, and he immediately departed to fetch the scytale, along with a pile of spare cleaning cloths from the scullery.

As soon as he returned, Sir Francis went to work wrapping the cloths around the wooden cylinder, pausing at regular intervals to check the expanding diameter with his measuring stick.

'Success!' he pronounced at last. 'The diameter is now exactly two and a quarter inches. Hold these cloths in place, Tom, while I wind the paper around it. We shall soon see how far-fetched my theory is…'

His cheeks flushed, his breathing a little heavier than normal, Sir Francis began carefully twisting the strip of paper around the cylinder. This was a matter of pride for him – Tom could see that. His reputation was at stake, and he wanted to prove to Cecil that he was still just as brilliant as ever.

Tom swallowed as he gripped both ends of the cylinder, one hand on either side of the slowly coiling ribbon of paper. He looked at the letters as they began to appear alongside each other, searching for anything recognisable as a word.

And then, quite suddenly, he saw one… The word he saw was P L A G U E. An ominous word. A threatening word. But a word all the same. Sir Francis had been vindicated. His 'far-fetched' theory had proved correct!

Tom showed them the word, and Sir Francis allowed himself a small satisfied smile. Cecil merely nodded. Then the three of them watched and waited for the full message to reveal itself. The more they read of it, the more shocked they became.

Chapter 15

Snakes in the Forest

STRATFORD–UPON–AVON, 8TH MAY 1603

The wind gusted down Chapel Street, blowing the discarded playbills into chaotic piles like autumn leaves, as the wagons of the King's Men began to roll out of town. Three generations of Shakespeare women were there to see them off, along with a scattering of townsfolk – the young, the curious and the idle – all waving enthusiastically. From a nearby church tower came the raucous clanging of a bell, as a line of solemn, black-clothed Puritans made their way to worship.

'This place is the back of beyond,' scowled Gus Phillips as he surveyed the scene from the front wagon.

'It's full of boors, churls, bumpkins and, worst of all, Puritans. If I come back here in twenty years, it'll be far too soon!'

'Fie on you, Mr Phillips, it's not so bad!' said Alice, seated next to him. 'Look at those people waving at us. We never had such a send-off when we left Southwark.'

'Nay, they were all too busy burying their plague-dead,' said Gus drily.

Will, seated on Alice's other side, had been unusually quiet so far this morning. 'How are you feeling, Mr Shakespeare?' she asked him.

'Sad and relieved,' he said. 'Wishing to tarry, yet happy to be gone. This place has been a dark cloud in my heart for so long – yet even a dark cloud can, when crested by the sun, present a silver lining.'

The sun, Alice guessed, was his daughters, but she did not say so. She understood Will was a private man, and he often spoke in riddles and metaphors as a means of keeping other people at bay. Instead, she turned her attention to the passing scenery.

The wagons, creaking along the muddy road, rolled past the poorer dwellings on the western side of town. They passed dunghills and vegetable gardens, thatched outhouses and orchards of apple, pear and cherry. They passed henhouses, pigsties, barns and fields of cows and sheep, before finally slipping into the shadows of the Forest of Arden. The deeper they ventured into the forest, the denser the trees grew around them. Branches formed an arch overhead, dimming the light and causing goosebumps to form on the arms of the travellers.

'I don't like forests,' shivered Robert Armin.

'Give me a London street any day, no matter how polluted,' agreed Gus.

'It's a far cry from the romantic forest in *A Midsummer Night's Dream*, eh Will?' said Richard Burbage. And he launched into Oberon's famous speech:

I know a bank where the wild thyme blows,
Where oxlips and the nodding violet grows,
Quite over-canopied with luscious woodbine,
With sweet musk-roses and with eglantine:
There sleeps Titania sometime of the night,
Lull'd in these flowers with dances and delight;

These words, spoken in Burbage's rich, mellow voice, cheered everyone up. Everyone, perhaps, but Will, who continued the speech in a much harsher tone:

And there the snake throws her enamell'd skin,
Weed wide enough to wrap a fairy in:
And with the juice of this I'll streak her eyes,
And make her full of hateful fantasies.

'Oh, Will,' groaned John Heminges. 'Did you have to mention that part with the snake and all? Burbage had put me in such a peaceful state of mind.'

'Every forest has its snakes, John,' said Will.

As he said this, there arose a sudden fearful commotion outside. Their horse neighed and the wagon drew up with such a jolt that its passengers were thrown right off their benches. This panicked all the horses and drivers to the rear, causing more neighing and cries of alarm as the convoy came to an abrupt and disorderly halt.

'God's Teeth! What is the meaning of this?' cried Gus, picking himself up off the floor. Then he glanced through the opening at the front of the wagon and began to tremble. 'Curses!' he breathed. 'Highwaymen!'

Alice, who had been pitched onto her knees, looked up and saw two men on horseback facing their wagon. The long barrels of their pistols were pointing at the driver, a hired man called Jack Bird, who was cowering in fright with his hands raised.

'They must want money!' whimpered Henry Condell.

'Then they're robbing the wrong people,' bleated John Heminges.

'What do you want of us?' cried Gus. He tried to sound defiant, but the crack in his voice betrayed his fear. When the highwaymen remained silent, Gus continued in a more pleading tone: 'We're only a band of poor travelling players. We have little money, a few costumes. Take it all, if you must. But please spare us our lives.'

'We don't want your money or your costumes!' said one of the highwaymen. He was a big man with a ruddy face, long hair and a bushy beard.

'What then?' demanded Gus.
'We want... William Shakespeare.'

Chapter 16

Shakespeare?

YORK HOUSE, 8TH MAY 1603

Tom, Sir Francis and Lord Cecil stared in silence at the message revealed by the scytale…

Plague in London. King's Men will tour. After Stratford-upon-Avon, they will enter the Forest. Capture Shakespeare here.

'I–I don't know what to make of it,' stammered Sir Francis after a moment. 'Why the devil would he want to capture Shakespeare? How could a playwright help their cause?'

'I've long suspected Shakespeare of being a papist,'

declared Cecil. 'He has far too many likeable Catholic characters in his plays. Friar Laurence in *Romeo and Juliet* to name but one. I also recall a reference to purgatory in *Hamlet* – very *un*-Anglican!' Cecil scratched his chin as he mentally developed his case against Shakespeare. 'Then there's his mother, Mary Arden, a member of a very well-known recusant family. Indeed, one of her relatives was executed for hiding a priest. As for his father, wasn't he fined once for refusing to attend a Church of England service? Oh yes, I wouldn't be a bit surprised if all the Shakespeares were secret papists.'

'That doesn't explain why they'd want to capture him,' pointed out Sir Francis. 'Why not simply recruit him, if he's such a papist?'

Cecil muttered something inaudible and went back to scratching his chin. He was as mystified as the other two, but didn't like to admit it.

'There's something else I don't understand,' said Tom. 'How did Father Watson know the King's Men were going to Stratford? I remember George, the wine boy at the Anchor tavern, saying they'd only decided to go there the afternoon before, which would have been the first of May, the same day Father Watson wrote the note...'

'Extraordinary!' said Sir Francis. 'There must be a spy within the King's Men, feeding Watson information.'

'That would not surprise me,' said Cecil. 'One of their hired men, Edmund Squires, was behind the plot to kill me two years ago. The entire company is most likely a hotbed of Catholic radicalism. Perhaps Shakespeare himself is the informant.'

Sir Francis chuckled at this. 'So Shakespeare told Watson he's going to Stratford and would Watson mind arranging for him to be captured as he's leaving. But would he not have preferred to be captured *before* he reaches Stratford – *if* the rumours of his troubled marriage are to believed?'

'Do you have any better ideas?' growled Cecil, riled by the philosopher's mocking tone.

'Maybe I should ride out there and warn them,' said Tom.

'It's probably too late for that,' said Sir Francis. 'They set off a week ago. Shakespeare may have already been captured.'

'Besides, it's vital we don't let them know that we're intercepting their messages,' added Cecil.

Tom knew all this. Even so he ached to climb astride Gunpowder and gallop back to Warwickshire. He feared for Alice's safety in the dark forest. What if she tried to play the hero and rescue her friend Will? She might end up getting captured herself – or killed...

Chapter 17

kidnapping a Playwright

THE FOREST OF ARDEN, 9TH MAY 1603

'Hand over Shakespeare, and no one will get hurt,' said the bushy-bearded highwayman.

The players in the lead wagon stared at him in horror.

'Wh-Wh-Why?' Gus managed, finally, to ask.

'Never mind about *why*, you clay-brained hedge-pig,' said the other highwayman, waving his pistol at Gus. 'Just push him out of the wagon, and then we'll let the rest of you go.' This one was taller than his companion, with dark, angry eyes and a pointed beard.

Alice felt herself trembling. She glanced at Will. He seemed astonishingly calm, almost resigned.

'No!' she cried, her voice shaking. 'No, this can't

happen!' She turned on Gus. 'Tell them, Mr Phillips. Tell them we're *not* going to let them take him!'

The others in the wagon instinctively turned to Gus, but he refused to meet anyone's gaze. His lips were dry.

'I'm losing patience,' growled the pointy-bearded highwayman. 'Hand him over, or I'll start shooting you one by one, starting with this fellow!' He trotted up and grabbed Jack Bird by the collar. The hired man uttered a terrified yelp as he felt the cold muzzle of the highwayman's pistol against his neck.

'Rest easy, gentlemen,' said Will Shakespeare. 'I am coming to you now.'

Alice stifled a sob, watching her friend step down into the road. Both highwaymen eyed him carefully as he walked towards them, hands raised clear of his body.

Pointy Beard released his hold on Jack Bird. 'How do we know it's him?' he hissed at his companion.

'Methinks it is,' said Bushy Beard. 'He bears a strong likeness to the portrait I saw.'

'Are you certain?'

'Gentlemen, I assure you I am Shakespeare,' said Will. 'I could stand here and recite all one hundred and fifty-four of my sonnets if it would convince you, or, to save time, you can take me at my word. Now what, pray, do you want with me?'

'This!' said Pointy Beard, and he trotted up to the playwright, raised his arm, and clouted him hard across the head with the butt of his pistol.

Will collapsed to the ground.

'No!' screamed Alice.

Even Bushy Beard paled at this savage act. 'Careful, old chap,' he gulped. 'We need him alive and, you know, compos mentis.'

Pointy Beard ignored his partner. He dismounted and raised the unconscious Will to his feet, then heaved him onto the back of his horse. He was climbing back into his saddle when Alice suddenly sprang out of the wagon and started trying to pull Will off the horse.

'You can't take him, you can't!' she wept.

Pointy Beard swung his fist, catching Alice on the jaw and sending her sprawling. Then he and Bushy Beard began cantering away. Alice clambered groggily to her feet and sprinted after them, but the kidnappers picked up speed, accelerating to a gallop until they had disappeared in a cloud of dust.

'There was nothing we could do,' Gus said to Alice as she returned full of anguish to the wagons.

'I'm not going to leave him to the mercy of those men,' she said bitterly, and she began unhitching the horse from the front wagon.

'Wait, what are you doing?' cried Jack Bird. But before he or anyone could stop her, Alice had unyoked and mounted the horse and began galloping away down the road.

'What are we supposed to do now?' she heard Gus cry as she sped away from them.

'You'll survive, Mr Phillips,' she muttered under

her breath. 'You always do!'

Alice had learned to ride with Richard. Mr Armin, in his spare time, looked after a couple of palfreys for an ostler at an inn in Bermondsey, and he sometimes let Richard and Alice ride them. Being back in the saddle reminded her of their jaunts into the woods around Camberwell. She could hear her brother's laughter as he raced her along the bridleway. Now, the drumbeat of her horse's hooves made a hollow, empty sound as she galloped along the lonely road.

After a quarter hour of hard riding, she came to a fork in the road. Fresh hoofprints indicated the kidnappers had taken the northerly fork, and she followed it. Several miles on from there, the hoofprints veered onto a narrow track. Alice charged up it, and suddenly had to pull hard on the reins, bringing her mount to an abrupt halt. Up ahead was a gate set within a high stone wall. A guard was closing the gate. He must have just now admitted the kidnappers and Will. Alice hastily led her horse off the track and behind a copse before the guard caught sight of her. She dismounted and tied the horse to a tree, then crouched down out of sight by the track side, watching as the guard headed back into his little hut. What sort of a place was this? Above the wall rose the battlements of a large gatehouse. It seemed a very grand residence for a pair of kidnappers. The name of the house had been inscribed in the stonework of the right-hand pillar. Peering more closely, Alice managed to make out the words: 'Bradenstoke Hall'.

Her mouth fell open in surprise. Bradenstoke Hall was the place Tom was supposed to take that message to. So the men who kidnapped Will were accomplices of Father Watson, and possibly also the kidnappers of Lady Arbella. Her heart began to beat faster at this thought. *Lady Arbella could be behind that wall…*

But why did these people want Will? What possible role could he play in a plot to overthrow the king? Alice didn't actually care much what they wanted him for. Her only desire was to rescue him, and Lady Arbella, too. And if anyone had the skill to break into this property undetected, it was her.

She returned to the horse and watched it munching peacefully on some weeds. If anyone approaching or leaving the house found it there, they'd know there was an intruder. It was too much of a risk leaving the horse here. She untied it and hissed: 'Git! Git!', smacking its hindquarters. The horse trotted away along the track in the direction they'd come. She hoped it would find its way back to the road where it might be discovered by the King's Men.

After watching the horse disappear around a bend in the track, she headed deeper into the forest, then began moving stealthily from tree to tree, making her way slowly towards the boundary of Bradenstoke Hall.

Chapter 18

The Torch Song

SOUTHWARK, 9TH MAY 1603

Sir Griffin Markham's reply to Father Watson was very brief, and quickly and easily decoded by Sir Francis. However, what it said was even more significant than Watson's message – at least in Cecil's view. The message read:

Very good. We have the other prisoners.

'The "other prisoners" must be this Richard fellow and Lady Arbella,' declared Cecil with a glimmer of triumph in his eyes. 'This confirms it! But we won't launch a rescue attempt yet. There are still too many unanswered questions: Who else is involved in the plot? What are their plans? And what do they want Shakespeare for? We will learn more, and spread our net wider, if we continue with our surveillance for a while longer. That means you, Tom. You must return to the Clink and hand Watson the reply from Markham. We can only hope that Watson will then dispatch you back to Bradenstoke with a fresh message.'

That afternoon, Tom, accompanied by Cecil's agent, Robert Poley, took a boat from York House to Southwark. They had docked their boat and were walking towards the Clink along a narrow cobbled street when Poley suddenly stopped and stared at Tom: 'Look at you, young man. You're wearing your servant's attire.'

Tom looked down and realised it was true – he'd forgotten to change into the dirty old shirt and leggings he'd worn last time. He'd donned these clothes unthinkingly upon his return to York House that morning. Perhaps fortunately, this was his older, shabbier servant's outfit – a jerkin and breeches he usually wore while assisting Sir Francis with his experiments – so it wouldn't look too out of place in a prison.

'How will you explain it to Watson?' Poley wondered.

'I'm not sure.'

Poley furrowed his brow for a moment, then brightened as an idea came to him: 'Tell him you used to be a servant to a recusant Catholic, and he allowed you to keep the outfit when he was sent to the Tower.'

Tom nodded. 'Watson'll like that story.'

'Aye,' chuckled Poley. 'It'll fit his view of a world divided between noble, generous Catholics and wicked Protestants.'

He strode up to the prison entrance and knocked. A small flap opened in the door and a pair of bloodshot eyes peered out.

'Ah, it's you, sir!' said Kendrick.

Bolts were drawn back and the door swung open.

'Welcome back, me old mates,' grinned Kendrick, flashing his gold tooth at them. He winked at Tom. 'Been missing Church services again, 'ave we, young man? Naughty! Well come on in, sir. Don't be shy!'

Tom bid farewell to Poley, and followed Kendrick into the prison. As before, he found himself assaulted by foul smells as he followed the gaoler down the steps and along the gloomy subterranean corridor, past cells of desperate prisoners. Father Watson was at prayer when they arrived at his cell. He turned as they entered and, to Tom's relief, looked delighted to see him.

'You have a message for me, do you, Tom?' he said eagerly as soon as Kendrick had left them. He didn't exhibit surprise at Tom's clothes, nor show any interest in how Tom had got himself rearrested.

'Aye, Father,' said Tom, extracting Markham's roll of paper from within his jerkin and handing it to him.

Watson pulled the roll open with a sharp snap and

briefly scanned the message, though it couldn't have meant anything to him in its encrypted form. 'I'll look at this later,' he said with a sidelong squint at Tom, and he stuffed it into his pocket. 'So you managed to find your way to Bradenstoke Hall without any trouble?'

'Aye,' said Tom.

'Good, good. You were remarkably quick. You must have had a fine horse. Where did you get it from, I wonder?' For the first time, Watson took a closer look at Tom, and his clothing. 'I like the outfit you're wearing today, young man. Very fine. Excellent tailoring. I wonder how you came by it.'

Watson's unblinking stare unnerved Tom. He took a deep breath and said: 'I was groom to, uh – to Sir Christopher Blount, and he bequeathed me these clothes, and also one of his best horses.'

Blount was a good choice. A staunch Catholic, he was one of the Essex rebels, beheaded in 1601 for high treason. Tom could only pray Watson hadn't known him, or wished to talk about him, for Tom actually knew nothing about the man.

Watson nodded pensively, seemingly willing to accept the story without question. 'You are most fortunate,' he muttered. Reaching behind him, he plucked a flickering torch from its iron wall bracket. He brought the flame close to Tom's face. Tom backed away nervously.

'No need to be scared, boy,' said Watson. 'I merely wished to show you something. See this…' He held up the thick, round wooden base of the torch. 'It's exactly twenty-seven poppy seeds wide.'

Tom tried to keep his face blank and uncomprehending. 'I'm not sure I understand, Father.'

'It unlocks my messages,' smiled Watson. 'Gives them their voice, so to speak… So we can hear their song.'

'It does?'

This had to be a good sign. If Watson was telling him about the scytale code, he must really trust him.

'But perhaps you knew that already,' murmured Watson, as he began winding Markham's message around the scytale.

Tom's heart jolted. 'H-How would I know that? Sir Griffin told me nothing.'

'Of course he didn't,' Watson said, and he fixed Tom with a sudden, startling grin. 'I can *trust* Sir Griffin.'

Returning his gaze to the scytale, he read the revealed message. Then he ripped the roll of paper off the wooden base and fed it to the torch. The flame brightened as it greedily devoured its brief meal.

'Sadly,' said Watson, as he watched the message burn, 'I can't trust *you*, Tom.' As he said this, he threw his left arm around Tom's neck and squeezed. Tom tried to scream, but could only choke as Watson's arm pressed down very hard on his throat. Tom strained to suck air through his constricted windpipe, while trying to pull Watson's arm away.

'You're a spy, Tom,' Watson said, shoving the torch's flame closer to his face. Tom shrank from the heat, as he heard Watson say: 'George, the wine boy at the Anchor, told me everything. He's my eyes and ears on the street. Feeds me information by slipping messages through my ceiling grate. He was the one who told me the King's Men were going to Stratford. And he saw you meet your friend Adam at the back of the tavern and show him the message I gave you. The message I *trusted* you with! You're a spy, and a traitor to your religion, Tom. And the punishment for spies and traitors is always *death!*'

Chapter 19

In Father Watson's Grip

Watson's arm tightened until Tom thought his neck might break. He could hear his own desperate wheezing gasps as he tried and failed to drag air into his lungs. He was weakening. The fire was meltingly hot against his cheek. Dark spots had appeared in front of his eyes. This was it. He was nearing the end. Feebly he tried to pull Watson's arm away from his throat. But it was no use. The priest's grip was like iron. He was going to die, here in this squalid gaol. He felt his legs give way, splaying beneath him. Only Watson's neck lock was keeping him upright. His arms fell back, hands bouncing against his sides. As they did so, he felt something there, in his pocket. Some kind of lump.

Tom was losing consciousness. Yet somewhere in the very back of his mind, something stirred. A memory. Sir Francis was talking to him…

I want to create the brightest flash ever seen… I want it to rival a bolt of lightning, or a beam of sunlight as it strikes the eye…

By experiment, sir.

By experiment, indeed…

And then later, on the street. Alice.

Are you blind, Tom? … Why are you blind today?

Sir Francis went too far with one of his experiments. Look!

He reached into his pocket, and…

His pocket! He was wearing the same trousers.

Tom's hand fluttered back to life. Somehow he forced it into his pocket and his fingers closed around the alchemical powder.

His mind was slipping into darkness. He could no longer remember where he was or what he was doing – only that he needed air and wasn't getting any.

Powder? What was this powder doing in his hand? Ah yes! *A flash, brighter than the sun.* That would be a pretty thing to see before he died…

He raised his hand and, with the last of his strength, flung the powder into the torch flame. His eyes were closed by now, but even so, for just a second he saw the air behind his eyelids turn silver-white. This was followed by a deep howl of shock, and the horrific tightness around his neck faded. He felt himself falling. There was no pain as he landed, only bliss, as his throat opened enough to admit air – sweet, life-giving air – into his chest. His throat still felt horribly crushed. He curled up into a ball on the floor, rasping and groaning as he fought for each breath.

Dimly he was aware of the door opening and a prison guard rushing in, wielding a club. He opened his eyes a crack and saw through his tears the big, bear-like figure of Father Watson staggering blindly around the cell. The priest was making wild swipes with his torch as the guard tried to clobber him with his wooden stick. Watson got lucky, catching the guard on the side of the head with one of his swipes. The guard fell headlong onto the floor, out cold.

Watson felt his way across the room towards the sound of Tom's coughing, crashing into a chair as he came. Tom felt a powerful hand grasp the back of his collar, and he was hauled roughly to his feet. Watson began dragging him towards what he must have assumed was the cell door. Instead, Tom felt a bone-crunching impact as the blinded priest collided with the wall.

'Which way?' growled Watson. 'Tell me now, boy, or I'll start throttling you again.'

'To the right,' Tom croaked.

They made it through the door and on up the corridor. Then Watson tripped and went sprawling on the steps, but his grip on Tom never faltered. With a bellow of frustration, he got back to his feet and staggered up the stairs, with Tom bouncing along behind him like a rag doll. As they reached the top, they were confronted by another guard. Tom cringed as the guard came rushing towards them, swinging his poleaxe. But as the man was about to strike, he suddenly stumbled as if pushed from behind. Then he tipped forwards and fell head first down the steps to land in a dazed heap at the bottom. Tom was astonished to see a familiar figure now emerging from the shadows. It was George the wine boy. He must have pushed the guard down the steps. The boy, who was small and agile, leapt up onto Watson's shoulders in one smooth movement.

'Let me be your eyes, master!' he cried. 'I'll get us out of here!' He handed Watson the fallen guard's poleaxe.

Watson grunted his appreciation. 'Which way?'

'Forwards, master. Towards the light. See, where I left the big door open.'

'I see it – I think,' muttered the priest. Still dragging Tom along by the collar, he charged towards the entrance of the prison.

Before they got there, two more guards appeared.

'Swing to the right, master…' squeaked George. 'Now duck! … Now to the left!'

Watson swung and ducked and swung again. Tom heard horrid bone-cracking sounds, and in a few seconds the guards lay unconscious on the floor. Kendrick dashed out of his office at the commotion, and nearly got trampled as Father Watson rampaged through the lobby, through the prison entrance and out into the street.

He didn't stop running here, but continued charging headlong down the street, with George yelling instructions in his ear to avoid pedestrians, horses and street vendors. Watson barely heeded these, and Tom suffered a series of brutal collisions to his knees and his shoulder before the priest swerved into a narrow alley and came to a halt.

'Rest here, master,' said George. The three of them crouched down behind a pile of barrels, as Kendrick, followed by two of his guards, went haring past the alley entrance and on down the street.

'We're safe here, master – at least for a while,' said George.

Father Watson wiped tears from his eyes and tried to blink some sight back into them. He hauled Tom up before him, fist still clenched tightly around his collar. 'Zounds, boy! What was that ungodly flash you made?'

Tom felt bruised and battered from the countless impacts he'd received during his violent passage through the prison and the street. His throat was still very painful, and all he could manage by way of an answer was a weak cough.

'Well, no matter,' grunted Watson. 'Your demonic flash did the Lord's work by so enraging me I became an unstoppable force.'

'A force of nature is what you were, master,' said George.

'A force of God, you mean,' said Watson, grinning and rubbing his eyes. 'A dozen guards couldn't have stopped me breaking out of that prison while I was in such a temper.' His grip on Tom tightened. 'As for you, traitor...' He pulled his captive closer still, so their faces were mere inches apart. 'I brought you with me for a purpose. I need you to do something for me.'

Tom waited in a semi-daze for Watson to continue.

'I need you to tell your masters that my friends have abandoned Bradenstoke Hall and moved to Hesleyside Hall in Northumberland. Do you understand?'

'Aye,' wheezed Tom.

'Say it to me.'

'Your friends,' Tom rasped, 'have abandoned Bradenstoke Hall and moved to... Hesleyside Hall in, in Northumberland.'

'Do you swear you'll tell them that?'

Tom nodded.

'Tell me you swear it!'

'I swear it.'

'He's lying, master,' said George. 'I can see it in his face.'

Watson switched his grip from Tom's collar to his neck. Waves of agony shot through Tom's tender throat. '*No!*' he tried to say. It came out as a muffled squeak. He couldn't go through this again.

'That boy, Adam – I know you love him,' Watson whispered. 'George here saw him kiss you, didn't you, George?'

'I saw it, master. And tender looks passed between them.'

What were they talking about? Why mention Alice now?

Tom found it hard to concentrate. He felt his throat closing up again, and squeezed his eyes shut, trying somehow to endure the pain.

'I know Adam's a player with the King's Men,' continued Watson.

'Aye, with the King's Men,' echoed George.

'And now he's our prisoner,' said Watson. 'See, the day after you left for Bradenstoke, I sent George there. He must have arrived shortly after your departure. I sent him with new orders. I'm sure you know what the original message was. It gave them details of where to find Shakespeare, so they could capture him. In the new orders, I told them to seize Adam at the same time. They must have him by now, imprisoned at Bradenstoke, along with the playwright. If you betray me on this, Tom – if you don't tell your masters that my friends have moved to Hesleyside Hall – then I'll give them the order to kill Adam. Do you want that? The death of your friend? No? Then do your duty.'

Horrified by these words, Tom croaked, 'I will.'

Watson opened his hand, and Tom fell coughing to the ground.

'Now go!' cried the priest, shoving him in the ribs.

Tom staggered to his feet. Like a startled colt making a clumsy break for freedom, he began to run. He ran out of the alley and down the street, then down another street that took him to the river. Here he hailed a wherry-boat. It was only when he was out on the river, watching the waterman rowing with strong, steady strokes towards York House, that the turmoil in his head began at last to clear. He felt his neck. The waterman cast him a sympathetic glance. No doubt the bruising was already starting to show.

As the distance lengthened between himself and the monstrous priest, Tom started to feel calmer and less frightened. There were decisions he needed to make. What should he do next? What should he tell Cecil? What should he do about Watson? But one thought above all others kept circling through his head...

They have Alice.

Back in the alley, young George was looking a touch bewildered. 'But master,' he said, 'you never dispatched me to Bradenstoke Hall.'

'Indeed I did not,' muttered Watson, climbing to his feet. 'But what's important is that young Tom thinks I did, and now he believes his beloved is in danger. And so long as he believes this, he will do my bidding. Now find me a horse, boy. I want to be out of this city and on the road to Bradenstoke by nightfall.'

Act Four

Chapter 20

An Iron Nail

BRADENSTOKE HALL, 9TH MAY 1603

Richard lay on his side on the floor of his prison chamber. With infinite patience, he scraped the tip of an iron nail against the mortar above one of the bricks at the back of the hearth. Back and forth he went, gradually chipping it away. He'd been labouring at this task for two days now and had already made quite a deep trench. Soon he would start work on the brick's bottom edge, and then its sides. By then, hopefully, the brick would be loose enough for him to remove it.

All this would take time, but that wasn't a problem, for he had lots and lots of that. There were many hours to fill between the twice-daily visits by the guards when they brought him his meals and replaced his chamberpot. He didn't pine for company, being well used to solitude from his days in the forest. What he did miss – sometimes quite intensely – was the ability to range freely through the open air across large distances. Cooped up in this room, he felt himself growing weak in body and spirit. But he wouldn't allow himself to drift into apathy. He'd set himself a task: he would break through this wall behind the hearth and make contact with his fellow prisoner.

If he needed any motivation to persevere with this task, it came from the sounds he heard, now and then, coming through the hearth. Late in the evening, he would listen to her sad, murmured prayers. He wanted, at these times above all, to comfort her – to make her realise she wasn't alone. At other times she made what sounded like speeches, as if she was imagining herself in the presence of someone else – perhaps with the man she loved, or with one of her captors. Richard guessed this from her tone rather than her words, which were muffled and hard to make out. Sometimes, though, instead of speaking, she would weep. This was the worst sound of all, and when he heard it he would attack the mortar with a special fury.

Her name was Lady Arbella Stuart. He had discovered this four days ago from a young man – a stranger. He'd spotted him crossing the bridge, heading towards the gatehouse, and had tossed an apple into the moat to attract his attention. Hearing the splash, the young man had glanced up. His face was open and honest – a pleasant, trustworthy face, Richard had thought. When he had arrived at the door of his chamber, Richard had begged him to help him escape. But the young man had refused – too scared, most probably. Richard had been sad about this for a while, but not for too long. The young man had, after all, supplied him with the name of the woman next door. He'd asked about Lady Arbella Stuart, and Richard had known instinctively that this was his imprisoned neighbour.

Lady Arbella. It was quite a name, matching the melancholy beauty of her voice. He wanted to rescue her and take her to Edward Seymour, the man she loved. Richard had first heard her voice coming through the hearth on the evening he was incarcerated here, eight days ago. If he'd started digging then, he would certainly have broken through to her room by now. But it had taken him a long time to find a suitable tool. The guards were always careful to take away the knife or spoon they gave him for his meals, and there were no other useable implements to be found in this bare, cell-like room.

Eventually, he'd found the nail, standing slightly proud of a floorboard beneath his bed. It had taken him half a day and several blisters to dig it out with his fingers. The next challenge had been to hide his progress from the guards. He did this by moving his bed against the wall next to the hearth, hiding it from the view of the guards, who never advanced far beyond the doorway. When one of them asked him why he'd moved the bed, he explained it was because the dawn light shining in from the window hurt his eyes and woke him up. They seemed content with this, failing to note that his window faced to the north-west, well out of sight of the dawn.

Richard continued to scrape at the mortar with his nail – a very blunt nail it was by now. He yawned and wiped some mortar dust from his eye. Tiredness was fogging his brain. He hadn't slept well the night before, having been woken in the small hours by a dream. The dream was, once again, about the mysterious girl. She and Richard were in the forest, and this time she was dressed as a boy. There were wolves nearby, slinking through the shadows, just out of sight. The wolves loved to eat girls, and they knew, somehow – or they suspected – that she was a girl, despite her clothing. Richard felt protective towards her, and at the same time powerless to save her. It was a terrible feeling. And all the time, the wolves were getting closer...

There came a loud squeak as the door of his chamber suddenly swung open. Richard jumped at the sound. *The guards never came at this time!* He scrambled to his feet, shoving the nail into the pocket of his breeches.

Sir Griffin Markham was standing near the doorway, flanked by a guard. Markham smelled of the forest. He had dirt on his boots and his forehead gleamed with sweat. In his hand, he carried a large book.

'What were you doing down there on the floor?' he asked Richard.

'I, uh… Sometimes I like to sleep there,' Richard said falteringly. 'It reminds me of my days in the forest.' He positioned himself between Markham and the hearth, attempting to block his view of it.

Markham frowned. He came a little further into the room. Richard adjusted his stance, trying to keep the hearth out of the other man's sightline.

'You've been in here a week now,' said Markham. 'I hope you've had a chance to reflect on your situation and reconsider our request. Soon the day will come when we will have need of your services. For that you must be ready, physically and mentally, for the task. But first you need to commit to it spiritually.' He held up the book he was carrying. 'If you swear on this Bible that you will do our bidding, I will release you from this room right now.

Richard stared at Markham, then at the open doorway.

With a smile, Markham continued: 'You will be free to roam the house and grounds of Bradenstoke as far as the outer wall – always in the company of one of my guards, of course.'

Richard imagined himself strolling freely over distances far greater than the four and a half yards of his room. *Free to roam*. They were seductive words.

But how free would he really be, if he was only allowed

as far as the outer wall, and always in the company of a guard? He looked at the Bible in Markham's hand. Was he not merely exchanging one kind of prison for another? He would be their slave, forced to kill in the name of a god he did not believe in – all for the sake of a few extra yards of space. And what of Lady Arbella? With a guard following him around all the time, making contact with her would become impossible. How could he even think of abandoning her?

'Gramercy,' he said, 'but I would prefer to remain here.'

Markham raised his eyebrows in surprise. His cheeks flushed and his breath shortened. 'You know, I've been on your side all this time, Richard,' he said. 'I've argued the case for being patient with you when Sir Robert Catesby would much sooner have had you killed. In his view, you're either with us or against us, and he has no time for anything in between. I'm not sure how much longer I can continue arguing the case for keeping you alive if you refuse to cooperate. Think about it!'

He turned on his heel and walked out of the room.

Chapter 21

The Cold and the Wet

It didn't take Alice long to realise the huge challenge she faced in attempting to break into Bradenstoke Hall. From her position, perched high in a tree overlooking the wall, she observed that the house was surrounded by a wide, deep-looking moat. The only way across the moat was via a bridge, overlooked by numerous windows and a large gatehouse with intimidating battlements. Even if she made it across the bridge under cover of night, she would be confronted by guards and a portcullis at the gatehouse entrance. Was there any other way of gaining access to the house? If there was, she guessed it would involve her getting very cold and very wet.

She spent the rest of the day climbing trees to spy on the house from different angles, or scavenging mushrooms and berries in the forest for food. After sunset, as the sky dimmed and the first stars appeared, the portcullis descended and the gatehouse entrance was lit up by torches, illuminating a pair of guards bearing long, deadly halberds. Alice kept watch on the entrance for a further hour. When it was fully dark, she came down from her tree and scaled the wall on the western side of the property. As quietly as she could, she dropped down onto the bank of the moat and hastily took cover behind a thick bed of reeds she'd spotted earlier. Her heart beating wildly, she peered at the guards to see if they'd noticed her. They hadn't. She could hear the murmur of their voices as they chatted. They sounded relaxed.

In the reeds near where she crouched, she saw a nest where a mother duck was quietly cooing to her chicks. Alice felt strangely envious of them. How simple and problem-free a duck's life was. By contrast, Alice was far from home on a dangerous mission with precious little hope of success. Bradenstoke Hall was big, and she had no idea in which of its many rooms Will and Lady Arbella were being held. Even if she managed to get inside the house, how would she go about finding the prisoners? It was far more likely she'd end up a prisoner herself.

She was beginning to think this whole venture was a mistake, and perhaps it would be better if she left now and hurried back to London, where she could report Will's kidnap to Cecil. But then something caught her eye. In one of the upper-storey rooms a fire had been lit. Framed by its light, a silhouette appeared at the window – it was the profile of a man of medium height with a neat beard and a high forehead. Alice gasped, for she would know that profile anywhere. It was Will! Seeing him there filled her with a powerful surge of hope. Now she knew she'd been right to follow the kidnappers, and she was right to try and rescue him.

But how fortunate that he'd chosen that very moment to appear at the window. The timing was almost too good to be true. Had he seen her coming over the wall? Was he discreetly showing himself to her, so she would know where to find him? She could not discount this possibility. Will was a remarkably observant man. Those eyes of his never missed anything.

Feeling a lot more confident now, Alice began wading into the dark water. It was freezing! The moat's sludgy bottom sloped steeply downwards until she was up to her chest. The icy water sloshed beneath her clothing, making her shiver. It really was heart-stoppingly cold. Soon, she was up to her neck. She took a deep breath and let her head sink beneath the surface. Then she began to swim underwater, pushing with her arms in sweeping motions and kicking with her legs. She aimed for the wall on the western wing of the house, beneath Will's window.

Swimming was one of the few activities at which Alice had outshone her brother. On warm summer days, during their rides into Camberwell, they would sometimes tether their horses and take a cool dip in a small lake they discovered on the southern end of Dulwich Hill. Richard's style of swimming involved an awful lot of splashing without much forward progress. Alice, for some reason, was a natural in the water. She discovered a technique of moving her arms and legs in a synchronised manner that allowed her to move through the water with speed and grace. She always won their races, despite Richard's roguish attempts to impede her by grabbing her legs underwater and pulling her backwards.

After a dozen strokes underwater, Alice raised her head and took a gulp of air. Her waterlogged shirt and breeches had become immensely heavy, weighing her down and making every stroke an effort. As a result, she was already breathless. Glancing up at the gatehouse, she saw with relief that the guards remained oblivious to her. She was about halfway across the moat – just another twelve or so swimming strokes would see her to the wall of the house. Taking another deep breath, she sank beneath the surface and swam with all her might through the Stygian blackness. She emerged this time close to the wall. Here the shadows were deepest, and she was out of sight of the guards because the gatehouse jutted forwards from the house's front wall. The wall here had a talus – a sloping base where it met the moat.

Dragging her heavy arms out of the water, she grabbed onto the talus – then immediately slipped off again. She sank, swallowing a mouthful of the foul-tasting water as she did so. Coughing and spluttering, she clawed her way back to the surface. Much of the talus, she now saw, was covered in slippery green slime. Alice hauled herself further along the wall until she came to a slime-free patch and seized hold of that instead. Here, she rested a moment, catching her breath.

A few feet above her, just below the ground-floor windows ran two horizontal lines of bossed stones, standing proud of the wall. They would give her hands and feet something to grip onto during her ascent. But to reach them, she would first need to raise herself completely onto the talus. She brought her legs up one at a time, scrabbling to find purchase on the narrow, sloping base. Her clothes were so heavy with water, she felt twice her normal weight. Eventually she hoisted herself up there with the help of tiny toe- and fingerholds, which she found in the cracks between the stones.

Alice clung awkwardly onto the talus, shivering violently in her sodden, freezing clothes. Her hands were like stiff claws, aching from the strain of clutching onto such tiny crevices. How she wished she'd decided to fashion herself a raft out of timber and reeds, and float across the moat instead of immersing herself in it. Grimacing, she managed to raise her hands up to the lower line of bossed stones. Once she'd climbed onto these, she shuffled leftwards until she reached the sill of the window beneath Will's. One of the windows was partly open, and a dim glow of firelight came from within the room. Seated by the hearth of the room was a man. A large, muscular fellow wearing an olive-green doublet, he was clasping a cup very tightly in his fist. His eyes, staring into the embers, seemed to glitter with savage thoughts. With a shock, Alice recognized him as Pointy Beard — one of the kidnappers. This startled her so much, she lost her footing. Her feet scraped at the wall searching for purchase, as she desperately clung onto the sill with her fingers. Pointy Beard must have heard her, for he suddenly looked up at the window. Alice darted out of sight. At the same moment, her left foot managed to rediscover the ledge of bossed stones. She quickly shifted herself rightwards, away from the window.

From within the room, footsteps approached. Alice hardly dared breathe as she held herself tightly to the wall. The kidnapper's hand appeared at the window, and he pushed it wider open, nearly knocking Alice's elbow with its frame. His long nose and hairy chin appeared in profile as he stuck his head out of the window. If she'd had the nerve, she could have slammed it shut hard in his face. He'd be so stunned, it might give her time to scramble in through the window and overpower him. But it was too risky. His scream might attract guards, and then she'd be done for. Pointy Beard swivelled his head slowly to the right and then to the left, but he failed to see the shivering girl pressed very close to the wall, just inches away from him. Alice was becoming dizzy from holding her breath.

At last, he withdrew from the window, and she heard him plodding back to his chair. She exhaled with relief. Gazing upwards, she could see the stars beyond the gatehouse battlements looking down on her with steely indifference. It made her feel very lonely, as if no one cared if she lived or died. She switched her attention to Will's window, just above her, and the fireplace glow reflected in the window panes became her beacon. Lifting her feet onto another line of rough-cut stones, she levered herself upwards. She moved slowly as she climbed, placing each hand and foot carefully, knowing one slip would send her splashing back into the moat.

Within minutes she was outside Will's window. She peered in – and there he was! He was seated by the fire, just like Pointy Beard, only Will was reading a book rather than clutching a drink. She was about to knock on the window when the door to his room suddenly swung open and a man entered, accompanied by a guard. It was the other kidnapper – Bushy Beard.

Chapter 22

Bless You, Window!

Alice quickly shifted out of sight. *What unfortunate timing!* She'd been looking forward to climbing in and warming her chilled, drenched body by the fire while she and Will made plans for their escape. She prayed Bushy Beard wouldn't stay too long.

Through the window, which was slightly ajar, Alice heard Bushy Beard speak. 'Will Shakespeare,' he said in a kindly voice. 'I am glad to see you risen from your bed. I trust my servants have seen to all your needs. Are you comfortable? How is your head?'

'My head is fine,' snapped Will. 'Except that it is in the wrong place – like the rest of me. Where am I and why have you brought me here?'

'I will explain everything in due course, Mr Shakespeare. But first, I would like to say how extremely honoured I am to make your acquaintance. You should know that I have long been an ardent admirer of your work…'

'In that case, I had sooner you had taken possession of my work and not my person,' Will responded. 'There are bound copies of my plays and poems available at all good booksellers' stalls, and at very reasonable prices. You could have enjoyed my work at your leisure without any inconvenience to me.'

'Pray forgive me for that inconvenience,' said Bushy Beard. 'I will shortly explain my purpose in bringing you here. But first let me introduce myself. I am Sir Griffin Markham, a former soldier, knighted by the late Earl of Essex. I was privileged to attend the Globe on that memorable occasion two years ago at the performance of your wonderful play, *King Richard II*.'

'You were one of the Essex rebels?' said Will.

'Aye.'

'Well, I thank God you were not successful that day. It would have besmirched my name to be associated with such a murderous rabble.'

Silence followed this remark, and Alice sensed a definite cooling of the atmosphere in the room.

When Markham finally spoke, he sounded a lot less friendly than before: 'I do not expect you to understand, Mr Shakespeare, the passions that drive men like me. Nevertheless, I cannot but be offended by your words.

We are not, and never have been, a *murderous rabble*. We are men of faith and principle, willing to fight, and die, for a better future for our country.'

'You are Catholics,' said Will.

'Aye.'

'And yet you supported the Protestant Earl of Essex.'

'We supported him because he promised us freedom of worship, and death to our oppressors. Unfortunately, Essex failed, and the persecution continued. Our hopes were raised when King James came to the throne, promising us toleration, but King James was a liar. The persecution has continued, worse than ever. These are desperate times for English Catholics, Mr Shakespeare. James might live another twenty years, and with two sons to succeed him and continue the persecution, there is every chance we shall be wiped out… unless we act now, before the king has a chance to establish his authority. Plans are already in place…'

'What plans? Do you intend to kill him?'

'We have a young man – deadly with a bow and arrow,' said Markham. 'When James reaches London, we will arrange for him to be killed, and for his cousin, Lady Arbella Stuart, to become queen.'

'Has she agreed to this?'

'She will become queen,' Markham repeated firmly.

Alice was finding it increasingly uncomfortable on her narrow perch just outside the window. The cold had penetrated deep into her bones. Her legs and shoulders were shaking, and now a sneeze was threatening. She risked removing her right hand from the window sill so she could squeeze her nose. This caused her to wobble, and she had to grip the wall extra hard with her left hand to prevent herself falling.

'So you have your assassin, and you have Lady Arbella,' said Will. 'Why do you need me?'

'We need you, Mr Shakespeare, to provide popular support for our... uh, *revolution*. The people of this country will naturally be disquieted by the death of their king. Your role is to prepare the ground, as it were, so when the deed is done, the public mood will be one of celebration rather than fear.'

Will laughed at this. 'Your faith in my influence upon the public mood is gratifying, Sir Griffin, and entirely fanciful. I am only a humble playwright...'

'You are far more than that, Mr Shakespeare,' Markham interjected. 'I have seen the people who attend your plays. You have the ear of bishops, nobles, shopkeepers and peasants. When your words are spoken, people stop and listen. I witnessed for myself how you had the audience enthralled that day two years ago. Imagine that effect repeated at inn-yards and playhouses around the city. If you write a play for us, redefining King James in the public mind, I will arrange for it to be performed on every stage in London.'

'You wish me to write a play for you?'

'Aye.'

Outside the window, Alice returned her hand to the

sill. The sneeze, thankfully, had receded. Fascinated as she was by the conversation within the room, she dearly wished it would end. Her feet and fingers were growing numb, and she wasn't sure how much longer she could remain clinging to this wall.

'What kind of play would you have me write?' asked Will.

'A play condemning King James as a villain and a usurper,' said Markham.

'I happen to rather like King James. He's a supporter of the arts, and the patron of our company.'

'For how long I wonder? He has the ear of the Puritans who wish to shut the playhouses down. As for Lady Arbella, her love of the theatre is genuine. She was a great friend of one of your heroes, the playwright Kit Marlowe, in her youth. Our interests, Mr Shakespeare, are more aligned than you might think.'

'And what if I refuse?'

Markham sighed. 'Then I'm afraid you will die here, sir.'

A bleak silence followed this threat. Alice shuddered. *Just agree to do it, Will,* she silently pleaded. *Or tell him you need some time to think about it, and could he leave you in peace, so I can get off this freezing wall!*

Then suddenly, her need to sneeze returned, more powerfully than ever. Alice desperately twitched and wrinkled her nose, but it was too late.

'*Aaa-chooo!*'

The sound seemed to echo like a gunshot for miles.

'What was that?' she heard Markham exclaim.

Alice wished she could shrivel away to nothing, or turn into a patch of lichen on the wall. She tensed her shoulders and closed her eyes, resigned now to being caught.

Then Will said: 'I pray your pardon, sir. I sneezed.'

'But I thought it came from over there by the window.'

'Nay, it was I. Methinks sound moves strangely in this room. It may be due to the angles of the walls.'

'I'm convinced it came from…'

'The window?' laughed Will. 'Aye, perhaps the window sneezed. Bless you, Window. I thought you an eye upon the world. But perhaps you are a nose, too!'

He knows I'm here! Alice smiled to herself. *And he's attempting to save me with his quick wit. Bless you, Will!*

'I will reflect on what you say, Sir Griffin,' said Will. 'And you'll have my answer in the morning. Prithee, leave me now. My head is sore again and I have need of rest.'

'Until morning then,' said Markham.

With enormous relief, Alice listened to his footsteps recede and the door open and close. Seconds later, the window opened and Will was there, beaming at her.

Chapter 23

This Is My Escape

Alice was so stiff with cold she could barely move, and Will had to help her into the room. 'My dear Adam!' he said in a low voice. 'You should not have risked your life like this.'

'I c-couldn't b-bear to see you t-taken away,' said Alice through chattering teeth as she warmed herself by the fire. A puddle had formed around her feet from the moat water dripping off her.

'You'd better take off those wet clothes,' Will advised. 'My hosts have provided me with some spare outfits. Please help yourself.'

Alice used the open door of a large wardrobe to give herself some privacy as she hurriedly changed.

'We have to find a way out of here, Mr Shakespeare,' she said, pulling on a rather baggy pair of hose and an outsize linen shirt.

'So long as it's not the same way you arrived,' he replied. 'You won't see me in that moat, Adam. I'll end up like Hamlet's girl.'

'Drowned, drowned,' giggled Alice, quoting the play. 'Too much of water hast thou, poor Ophelia, And therefore I forbid my tears.'

She was happy to be warm and dry again, and with her friend. They would find a way out of here – somehow.

But her relaxed cheerfulness was short-lived, for just then the door burst open again. Alice leapt inside the wardrobe and quietly closed the door.

'Sir Griffin!' she heard Will exclaim. 'Why have you returned? I told you, I wished to rest.'

'I thought I heard voices in here,' said Markham suspiciously.

Through a crack between the two wardrobe doors, Alice observed Markham march across the room and throw open the window. He leaned right out and looked carefully all around.

'Take care, sir,' said Will. 'If that window sneezes again, you could fetch up in the moat.'

Markham closed the window and turned on Will, the furrowed lines on his forehead demonstrating how little he cared for the playwright's attempt at humour. 'Has someone else been in this room?' he demanded.

'Aye,' said Will nonchalantly.

Markham tensed – as did Alice. *What kind of game was he playing?*

'King James was here just now,' said Will, 'together with Lord Cecil, and the Earl of Essex, who was looking in less than perfect health, what with his lack of head. Anyway, it was quite a party.'

Markham's frown deepened. 'Be serious, sir. My patience is wearing thin. Have you or have you not been visited here?'

'If I have, it is only by characters I've been fashioning in my imagination. It helps me sometimes to speak them – in different voices. That is no doubt what you heard. I already have a few ideas about this play you wish me to write...'

'Yes, about that,' said Markham. 'I have an idea of my own. Perhaps I can tell you about it.' He seated himself in Will's fireside chair.

'By all means,' said Will, with a glance towards the wardrobe. 'So long as it doesn't take too long. I am, as I said, rather tired.'

'Of course, of course,' said Markham. 'It's a simple enough idea, but, I think you'll agree, rather a good one.' He leaned back and put his feet up on a footstool. 'It goes without saying that we cannot directly criticise King James in our play, or it would never receive a license from the Master of Revels. Yet I believe I have found a figure in history who will be recognised by almost everyone, except the censors, as representing the king.'

'And who might that be?'

'Otho.'

'Otho?'

'Aye, he was a Roman emperor. I don't expect you've heard of him. He wasn't one of the famous ones. He reigned for just three months in 69 A.D., a very chaotic time in the empire. Yet I've noticed that he and James have a great deal in common. Like our king, Otho had a deformity in his legs – he was splay-footed and bandy-legged. Otho also had a reputation for extravagance and recklessness – criticisms that have been levelled at our present monarch. And, like James, he ruled a divided realm threatened by civil war. Otho was 38 when he died; James is 37, and if our plan succeeds, he, too, will be 38 when he meets his death. The audience cannot fail to see the parallel.'

After a pause, Will said: 'I will need to do some research.'

'My library is at your disposal.'

'Do you have *Plutarch's Lives*?'

'Aye. And Suetonius, and Juvenal, all of whom make mention of Otho.'

'Good,' Will said. 'Then I shall write your play.'

'Excellent!' declared Markham. 'I will arrange for a desk and writing materials to be brought to your room in the morning.'

Alice was pleased that Will was pretending to play along – their escape would be easier if it wasn't expected. As soon as she heard Markham depart, she jumped out of the wardrobe.

'You played him like a lute, Mr Shakespeare,' she smiled.

Will nodded. 'He has the arrogance of a Caesar, and the deluded nobility of a Brutus. I have written about such characters, and I know how their minds work.'

'Of course you do! And while you pretend to start work on this play, we can plot our escape. Perhaps when you're in the library you can check if there's a way out through a window…'

'Escape? Adam, I cannot think about escaping now.'

Alice stared at him. 'You joke surely!'

Will's expression did not suggest he was joking. '*This…*' he said, indicating the space around him, 'is my escape. It's my chance to get away from Gus and the gruelling demands and sheer tedium of the tour. My only reason for agreeing to go was so that I could see my family again, which I've done. Now, by happy accident, I've been granted an opportunity to do what I love most – to write. Here in this tranquil setting – with access to a *library*! It's a playwright's paradise.'

Chapter 24

From Otho to Othello

Alice already knew that Will was prepared to sacrifice a great deal in pursuit of his art, including regular contact with his family. Even so, his words were a great shock to her. 'Happy accident?' she cried. 'These men are evil! They've kidnapped an innocent woman, and plan to kill the king. How can you even consider writing a play for them?'

'I won't be writing it for *them*,' he responded calmly.

'Even so, you know they'll use it for their own foul purposes. They'll make sure people see the parallels between Otho and James. Your play will forever be associated with the murder of a king.'

'I'm not going to write about Otho,' said Will.

'But you said…'

'I know. But I have another, much better idea. I'll

convince Sir Griffin of its merits, have no fear. I'll make him think it's all about James, but it won't be. It'll be about so much more than that.'

He picked up the book he'd been reading and offered it to her. Intrigued despite herself, Alice took it and opened it to the title page. She read aloud: '*Hecatommithi* – by Cinthio'.

'It's a collection of stories written by an Italian,' said Will. 'I brought it with me on the tour to read. One of the stories is about a brave and handsome Moorish general, married to a beautiful woman called Desdemona. He has an ensign, or chief officer – a wicked man, determined to destroy the general. The ensign plants the idea in the general's mind that Desdemona is being unfaithful to him with one of his captains. The ensign concocts false evidence to this effect, and in a fit of jealous rage, the general murders Desdemona. Only then does he realise that the ensign had been lying and she was entirely innocent. Stricken with grief, the general kills himself.'

'It sounds very sad,' said Alice.

'It will be, when I write my version – unbearably so.'

'But how will you convince Sir Griffin that it's about James?'

'That's the clever part,' smiled Will. 'It will all be in the names I give the characters. Cinthio doesn't give any of his characters names, except for Desdemona. So I'm free to name them as I please. Sir Griffin may appreciate a reference to Otho – so I could call the

Moorish general Otho...'

'But Otho was bad,' Alice pointed out.

'Not in the way I'd have written it – misled perhaps... Even so, you're right. The two characters are too different. I suppose I could change it slightly to... Oth*ello*?'

'That has a certain ring to it,' said Alice.

Will began pacing the room, head bowed in thought. 'As for the wicked ensign, I'll need to call him something a *little* like James, to keep Sir Griffin happy. How about Jacob – Latin for James?'

'It's too obvious,' said Alice. 'Everyone will know who you mean.'

'Then I could translate Jacob into another language. In Spanish, for example, it's Iago.'

'That sounds much better,' said Alice. 'But I'm still not sure you'll convince Sir Griffin that it's the right play for his purposes. It's not about a bad king destroying his country, is it? It's about love and jealousy.'

Will pondered this, while continuing to pace the room.

'I'll tell him it's an allegory,' he said at last, '– with all the characters representing different things. So Iago is King James, and he persuades Othello, who represents England, to kill Desdemona, who represents the English Catholics. He does this by falsely accusing her of infidelity with the captain, who represents Rome.'

'So you mean James is telling England that its Catholics are secretly loyal to the Pope?'

'Aye, something like that. And the play will end with Othello's suicide. In other words, James will, by his actions, cause the downfall of England... It's all nonsense, of course – but Sir Griffin will love it.'

'I'm sure he will,' said Alice, observing the spark of amusement in Will's eye. She was pleased for him. He was clearly excited to be embarking on this project. Yet she couldn't help feeling somewhat aggrieved. 'I risked my life coming here, for nothing,' she murmured.

Will's smile vanished. 'I'm grateful – truly I am,' he said earnestly. 'You are a *friend*, Adam, and I do not use that word lightly. But… I did not ask you to come.'

'I know that,' said Alice, looking down. 'And I'm not angry. I know you must do this. But there is another person imprisoned here who will perhaps be more appreciative of my offer of help.'

'Lady Arbella?'

'Aye. I will see if I can find her and get her away from here.'

'Good luck with that,' said Will.

Alice returned the book to him, then began moving towards the door. Before reaching for the handle, she hesitated as a thought occurred to her, and turned back to Will. 'Mr Shakespeare, Sir Griffin has given you the freedom of the house, has he not?'

'He's offered me the use of the library, which isn't quite the same thing.'

'Aye, but he didn't tell you where the library was. So no one would be too surprised to see you poking around the upper corridors, opening doors and checking rooms. And if they challenge you, you could always say you were looking for the library.'

'If challenged, I'll play the fool just as well as Robert Armin. But what you really want is for me to find Lady Arbella for you. Am I right?'

'What I want is for you to scout the upper floor, so you can tell me if there are any guards around and where they are, and which rooms Lady Arbella definitely isn't in. And, yes, if you happen to stumble upon her, you could tell me that, too!'

Will smiled. 'I'll be your spy,' he said. 'But I draw the line at hiding behind any tapestries. You get the point?'

Alice did. Will was referring to a scene in *Hamlet* when Polonius spied on the prince and his mother by hiding behind a tapestry, and was then stabbed to death by Hamlet.

'No tapestries,' she promised.

She watched him leave, then went and sat down on his bed. It was close enough to the wardrobe to enable her to scurry in there again if Markham or someone else happened to come in.

The minutes ticked by, and Alice felt an unexpected tiredness sweep over her. *Where had Will got to?* Soon she was no longer sitting on the bed, but lying on it. Her mind became sluggish. The swim and climb had really taken it out of her. But she couldn't allow herself to fall asleep. She must remain alert, in case someone came in. The bed was so comfortable, though.

It wouldn't hurt to close her eyes, just for a moment…

'Adam! Wake up!'

Her eyelids fluttered open. It was Will staring down at her. *Thank goodness!*

She sat up. 'Forgive me, Mr Shakespeare,' she said, sliding off the bed. 'I was so tired, I… How long have I been asleep?'

'Never mind about that,' he interrupted. 'I have good news.'

'What is it?'

'I have found Lady Arbella. She's in a room not far from here. I spoke to her just now, and told her to expect you.'

'Gramercy, Mr Shakespeare!' cried Alice, making for the door. 'Where can I find her?'

'Turn left in the corridor outside, go through two interconnecting doors into another corridor and her room is the first on the left. There are no guards there at present, but she says normally there are, so make haste.'

Alice slipped out of the room and tiptoed quickly along the corridor. It had to be very late by now and the house was silent. She opened the door at the end of the corridor and entered a room, which she guessed lay to the rear of the gatehouse. The door opposite, as Will had said, led to another corridor. She approached the first door on the left, feeling a pleasant tingle of anticipation. Taking a deep breath, she opened it.

The room was even more spacious and well-furnished than Will's. Standing on a rug near the hearth stood a petite, well-dressed woman in her late twenties. She had wide blue eyes, a high forehead and a small mouth. Her face, illuminated by the glowing ashes of the fire, was pale and tense. Her body seemed unnaturally still as she stared at Alice.

Something's wrong, Alice thought. *Why does she not move? She looks scared, almost horrified, by my arrival. Yet Will said she was expecting me.*

'Lady Arbella,' said Alice. 'My name is Adam. I've come to take you home.'

Still the woman didn't react – except, if anything, to appear more distressed. Her eyes widened. A tear trickled from her eye and ran down her frozen cheek.

'Is something the matter?' Alice asked.

The lady opened her mouth. 'Run!' she hissed.

As she said this, the shadows began to shift in the corners of the room. Figures emerged from their hiding places – men armed with long, sharp spears. Alice tried to back out of the room, but she was too late. Strong hands clamped down on her shoulders, preventing her from moving. Someone was behind her – he must have been hiding behind the door when she came in. She struggled against his grip, but he was too powerful. Two guards advanced towards her, training their cruelly sharp, iron-tipped halberds upon her neck. Lady Arbella, meanwhile, collapsed to her knees, weeping and praying at the foot of her bed.

The man clasping Alice's shoulders suddenly spun her around to face him. It was Pointy Beard – the tall kidnapper. He studied her from beneath hooded eyelids. 'You're the lad who tried to stop us taking Shakespeare today,' he said.

Alice stared back at him in sullen silence.

'Determined, aren't you?' he sneered. 'Swimming the moat, then scaling the wall. A pity for you that you sneezed, or you might have got in here unseen. Griffin told me about the sneeze and I investigated. I went into Shakespeare's room just now and saw you sleeping like a milk-fed baby on his bed, while he was in here chatting with Lady Arbella. I could have nabbed you then, but first I needed to know what you were up to. If you'd come here simply to rescue your friend the playwright, then why did the two of you not escape when you had the chance? Why did he go wandering around the house and fetch up here, talking to the princess? It made no sense. And then, in a flash, I understood – you've come to get her, too, haven't you? And you asked Shakespeare to find her for you. I know I'm right because you walked in here, fell right into my little trap... You came here to rescue her, didn't you?'

Alice kept her mouth shut, determined not to give anything away.

'Not very talkative, are you?' he smirked. 'Well, that's alright. We'll soon have you blabbing like a flap-mouthed tittle-tattler. Maybe then you can explain why a prentice player with the King's Men, a friend of Shakespeare, would want to rescue Lady Arbella...'

When Alice didn't respond, Pointy Beard merely nodded. 'Have it your way. But I'll get the truth out of you if I have to cut it out with my sword. And don't think your youth is any protection. The enemy is the enemy in my book, no matter what his age.' He turned to the guards. 'Take him to the castle dungeon.'

With that, Pointy Beard swept from the room. Alice felt the sharp tip of a halberd in the small of her back. 'Get moving!' said a gruff voice.

Chapter 25

Another Angle

YORK HOUSE, 9TH MAY 1603

Tom was no stranger to lying. He'd lied before, many times. During the Essex rebellion two years ago, he'd lied to protect his master, the Earl of Essex; he'd lied to thwart him, too, after he switched sides. These days, working as a spy for Lord Cecil, his whole life had become a lie. He had to pretend to be someone he wasn't – and he'd found, to his surprise, he was rather good at it. This didn't make him a bad person, in his view. As he kept telling himself, he was lying for his king and country, and there had to be some kind of honour in that.

But now, everything had become a lot more complicated. He was being asked to lie not by Lord Cecil, but by the enemy, Father William Watson. The priest wanted Tom to tell Cecil that his collaborators and their prisoners had moved to Hesleyside Hall in Northumberland. This wasn't any old lie Tom was being asked to tell – it was false information that could allow the enemy to slip the net and disappear altogether. It was a betrayal of the cause Tom had pledged to fight for. And yet, if he didn't do it, Alice would die.

So should he betray his country, or his friend? That was the question Tom was wrestling with as he returned to York House. He'd hoped to have some time to himself, to reflect on his dilemma. But Cecil was waiting for him there, in the library, when he arrived.

The chief minister was examining Sir Francis's orrery – a clockwork model of the Earth, sun, moon and planets. He was leaning over the mechanism, his nose virtually touching its gearwheels, as his hand twisted the key, winding the spring. When he let it go, his thin lips curled into a faint smile as he watched the heavenly spheres begin to rotate about the Earth.

'Funny thing,' he said, glancing up at Tom as he came sidling in through the door. 'I was talking about this with Francis the other evening at dinner, and he told me it's almost certainly all wrong.'

Tom, preoccupied with his predicament, was slow in responding. 'Wrong, my lord?'

'Aye. He says the Earth, along with the planets, should be going around the *sun*.'

'It's what Copernicus wrote, sire,' replied Tom. 'Sir Francis showed me his book. It's a very interesting theory…'

'Stuff and nonsense,' said Cecil, straightening. 'The sun goes around the Earth. I see it with my own eyes every day. Modern philosophers like Francis always like to over-complicate things. If they want to know how the world works, they should consult the classics. Men like Ptolemy and Aristotle. They knew a thing or two. Better that than looking through that seeing-tube of his and concocting new-fangled theories about the universe.'

'Sir Francis says that sometimes you need to look at things in a different way…' said Tom. 'It's like that painting of "The Ambassadors". You can't see the skull unless you look at it from another angle…'

He paused. *Another angle…* Maybe he needed to look at *his* problem from another angle. It didn't have to be just a simple choice between two equally horrible alternatives. The model could be wrong. The sun didn't have to move around the Earth. He could lie to Cecil, then fix the problem himself…

'Another angle,' muttered Cecil. He walked away from the orrery, hands clasped behind his back, and wandered over towards the window. 'There are no *good* angles on our current predicament, are there, Tom?' He turned, and fixed him with a dark, avian stare. 'From every angle, it's catastrophic. Poley's just told me that

Watson has escaped. Did you have anything to do with that? I'm guessing you did, because you were seen being dragged along behind him. What's that bruising on your neck? Did Watson do that to you?'

Tom swallowed. This was the moment of truth – or falsehood. If he told Cecil that Watson had attacked him for being a spy, then the Hesleyside Hall story would have no credibility, and he needed to give it credibility, or else Alice was doomed.

'His attack on me was a ruse, sire. He wanted to draw the guards into his cell, and it worked. One of them came in. Father Watson knocked him out, then escaped, dragging me along with him.'

That lie had been easy enough to tell. But one lie always gave birth to others, and everything would get messier...

Cecil pursed his thin lips, forcing uncomfortable words from his mouth: 'I'm sorry, Tom,' he said, 'for putting you through that. It can't have been pleasant. I knew Watson was dangerous, but I never thought he'd resort to assaulting a fellow recusant. What happened after that? How did you get away from him?'

'He let me go, sire. But before he did, he told me something. He told me the conspirators have moved out of Bradenstoke Hall. They're now at Hesleyside Hall in Northumberland.'

'What?!' Cecil's eyes widened to reveal the whites all around them. 'Did he say why?'

'Nay, my lord.'

The chief minister rubbed his beard, his brow creased with thought. 'I suppose they might feel more secure up there – close to the Scottish border, in case they need to flee. Which means they must know they're being watched. Or…' His face paled as another, much more alarming thought occurred to him. 'Or they could be planning a rebellion – another Rising of the North. They must be hoping the northern Catholic nobles will rally to Arbella just as they did to Mary Queen of Scots back in '69!'

Tom had never seen Cecil so grim-faced.

'The time for spy games is over,' he announced. 'I must go and speak to the king. We'll send an army to Northumberland, lay siege to Hesleyside Hall, demand the surrender of the conspirators, and then kill every last one of them.'

An army? What have I done? thought Tom. But it was too late to back out of his plan. Time was still on his side, for it would take days, if not weeks, for Cecil to raise an army and send them north. By then, Tom hoped to have crushed the conspiracy all by himself.

And yet, in another sense, time was very much against Tom – because Watson now knew that he was a spy and that Bradenstoke was no longer safe. Very soon, he would move the prisoners to another location, and that could be anywhere in the country – anywhere except Hesleyside Hall. Tom had to get to Bradenstoke before they abandoned it. Watson had probably already dispatched a message to them, or perhaps he was heading up there himself. To have any chance, Tom had to leave today.

Cecil was striding out of the library when he collided head-on with Sir Francis coming the other way. Both men looked stunned by the impact, especially Sir Francis, who began weaving around the room like a drunkard before collapsing on a chair.

'Can't you look where you're going, man?' cried Cecil, rubbing his forehead.

'Pray forgive me,' mumbled Sir Francis. 'I am… I am…' Then he toppled off his seat and collapsed onto the floor.

Tom rushed to his master's side. 'Sir! Sir! What ails you?'

Sir Francis stirred. His eyes fluttered open briefly, then closed again. He began to snore.

Cecil looked at him with disdain. 'Is he drunk?'

'Nay, my lord,' said Tom. 'I can smell no alcohol on his breath. He is… asleep.'

'Well, when he awakes, tell him I expect to see him tomorrow morning at the Palace for a meeting with the Privy Council. I bid you good day, young man.'

After Lord Cecil had departed, Tom fetched Owen the groom, and the two of them carried Sir Francis to his bed. Then Tom summoned Sir Francis's physician. The physician soon arrived and immediately set about examining the still-sleeping patient. He emerged a short while later, shaking his head.

'You say he walked into the chief minister,' he said,

'yet I can find no trace of bruising or concussion. His breathing is regular, as is his pulse. He shows all the signs of simply enjoying a good sleep. I cannot understand it. I've been your master's physician for fifteen years and never once has he complained of sleepiness during the day. Has he been working especially hard lately, or keeping irregular hours?'

'No more so than usual,' replied Tom.

'Then I am at a loss to explain it,' said the physician. He instructed Tom to inform him of any change in Sir Francis's condition, then departed.

Chapter 26

The Potion

Tom was anxious to leave for Bradenstoke as soon as possible. Yet he couldn't, in all conscience, abandon his master while he was in this condition. He suspected that a clue to Sir Francis's mysterious lapse into slumber might be found in his basement laboratory, and this was where he now headed.

The large table at the centre of the laboratory was in its usual disordered state, with flasks and vials of diverse shapes and sizes competing for space with teetering piles of books, a candlestick and writing materials. One of the flasks was filled with a colourless liquid. Tom picked it up and sniffed it. He felt a sudden rush of dizziness, causing him to stagger slightly and have to grab onto the edge of the table for support.

He put the flask down and backed away from it. *What had Sir Francis been playing at?*

A large book made up of plain sheets of paper, where Sir Francis recorded the results of his experiments, lay open nearby. Tom examined the most recent entry. The handwriting noticeably deteriorated towards the end: *Today,* Sir Francis wrote, *I have succeeded in duplicating the method invented by Valerius Cordus for synthesizing sweet oil of vitriol. I will now inhale the vapour of the solution and attempt to describe the resulting effects. I am starting to feel most...*

The remainder was an illegible scrawl ending in an ink blot. Next to this lay a broken quill. Tom had barely sniffed the solution, yet he was still feeling somewhat lightheaded. He guessed Sir Francis had inhaled it very deeply, perhaps more than once. In his stupefied state, he must then have crawled up out of the basement and stumbled through the house as far as the library before cannoning into Lord Cecil. It displayed, if nothing else, the man's remarkable stamina.

For how long would Sir Francis sleep? For hours? For a whole day? Tom had hoped to be on the road to Warwickshire by now. If he delayed much longer, he would be too late. Then an idea occurred to him. He ripped out a blank sheet from his master's experiment book, dipped a fresh quill in some ink, and began composing a letter to Sir Francis. The letter explained everything: about how Father Watson had discovered he was a spy, how he'd ordered him to tell his masters about the move to Hesleyside Hall, and then threatened to kill Alice (he called her Adam in the letter) if Tom didn't do as he was told. Tom then wrote of his intention to ride to Bradenstoke and rescue the prisoners being held there. When he signed the letter, Tom felt as though he was signing his own death warrant. For here was proof that he'd lied to the chief minister and abetted the enemy, thereby endangering the life of the king. These were surely acts of high treason, which could have but one consequence: an appointment with the hangman.

Tom melted a stick of red wax in a candle and let it drip onto the rolled-up letter to form a seal. His one hope lay in his mission to Bradenstoke. If he could rescue Lady Arbella, the plotters might just give up, and Tom could hope that the authorities would be persuaded to exonerate him. But if he failed, it would probably be better if he died in the attempt, or else fled into exile – for he would never be able to show his face in London again. In that eventuality, the letter would serve its purpose, because at least Sir Francis and Lord Cecil would know the truth, which would aid them in their efforts to defeat the conspirators.

'How now, Tom!' called a voice from the top of the basement steps.

Tom looked up and gave a start. Sir Francis was there, looking pale yet surprisingly clear-eyed.

'Sir, you should be a-bed,' Tom said, quickly stuffing the letter into his pocket.

'Nonsense, lad,' said Sir Francis, as he made his way, somewhat unsteadily, down the steps. 'I am in excellent health. Never better. I see you've discovered the cause of my temporary spell of somnolence.'

Sir Francis rounded the table and picked up the flask containing the colourless liquid, while keeping it well clear of his nostrils. 'Sweet oil of vitriol,' he said reverently, as if invoking the name of a goddess. 'Or, as I prefer to call it, *ether*.'

'It's dangerous stuff,' said Tom.

'Aye,' said Sir Francis proudly. 'I may have made a slight error with the recipe – too much sulphuric acid most likely. But there can be no progress without accident, can there, Tom? This might well be the most powerful sleeping potion ever created.'

'Sir,' said Tom, 'now that you're well, I would like to ask you something, if I may.'

'Hm?' said Sir Francis vaguely, his eyes and mind still on the potion.

'Might I ask you again, sir, for a few days leave, and the use of your horse, Gunpowder?'

Sir Francis put down the flask. 'Is this on Cecil's business?'

'Nay, sir.'

'Then what?'

Tom paused. 'It's just something I must do, sir. Forgive me, I cannot tell you, for fear of...'

'For fear of what?'

'For fear of compromising you, sir.'

Sir Francis became very still. He seemed almost to stop breathing. 'Are you going against Cecil, Tom?'

'Nay, sir!' Tom cried. 'I am Lord Cecil's loyal servant, as I am yours. But I also love my friend, Adam. And he is in grave danger, unless I act now.'

'I confess I'm a little confused, Tom. Why should I or Lord Cecil, or anyone, object to you saving your friend? What information are you concealing that you think might compromise me?'

Tom briefly closed his eyes and tried to compose himself. 'Sir, if I am successful in my mission, then I will have done my duty to my friend, and to my country – and you and Lord Cecil will have no cause for complaint. But if I am not… If I fail to return within the week, then there are some facts you must know, and share with Lord Cecil.' Tom took the letter out of his pocket and handed it to Sir Francis. 'It's all in here. But, I pray you sir, do not open it, nor tell anyone of the letter's existence, until then. It is my fervent hope that the letter will never need to be opened, and that upon my return, all being well, I can safely destroy it.'

Sir Francis looked closely at the letter, as if trying to divine its secrets through the furled paper. 'I am already feeling somewhat compromised, Tom. If it turns out that the letter contains vital intelligence, and I waited a week to…'

'You can tell Lord Cecil you only that day discovered it. The last thing I want is for this to damage you, sir. The fault is all mine, and you have been so kind to me…'

Tom had to stop as his voice was shaking. He felt his master's hand upon his shoulder. 'Say no more, lad. I understand you're in a difficult position. You have my word the letter won't be opened until a week from today.'

'God grant you mercy, sir.'

Sir Francis picked up the flask of ether and poured some of it into a small leather bottle. 'I don't know who or what you're likely to face on this little adventure of yours, Tom,' he said, screwing on the lid, 'but it can't hurt to take some of this. You never know, it might come in handy.'

Tom took the bottle. 'I don't know how to thank you, sir,' he said.

'Then don't waste time trying. Go now, my boy, and do what you must do. And I pray that fair fortune smiles upon you, and upon us all.'

Act Five

Chapter 27

The Space Between the Walls

BRADENSTOKE HALL, 12TH MAY 1603

In his dream, Richard and the girl were walking through the forest when they came to a large oak tree with a hollow near the base of its trunk. Richard placed his hand in the hollow and he pulled out a wooden box. Inside the box was a locket. For some reason, the locket was very precious to him. He rubbed his thumb over its finely engraved silver case, cherishing it. Then, using his thumbnails, he prised it open. Inside was a tiny painting of a woman's face. She was smiling at him. A warmth spread through Richard's chest as he gazed at her. It felt like he'd come home.

But when the girl saw what he was looking at, she dashed the locket from his hand. He flinched as it bounced and tumbled along the ground before coming to rest by a tree root. He stared at the girl. Why was she so angry? She stormed over to the locket and raised her foot as if about to smash her heel into the picture of the woman. Richard pushed her before she could, and she lost her balance and fell to the ground. The girl started to cry. She cried not because Richard had pushed her, nor because she was hurt by the fall. Richard knew the source of her tears lay much deeper, and it was all about the woman in the locket.

He woke up feeling both guilty and depressed, and found himself sprawled on the floor by the hearth. He must have fallen asleep here while he was digging. His body felt stiff and uncomfortable. His hands ached. There were red marks on his palms. The crying, he now realised, hadn't stopped with the end of the dream. He could still hear it coming faintly through the brickwork. The sound raised the hairs on the back of his neck. It was like a cold fist around his heart. He wished he could stop it.

Raising his eyes, he checked on the brick he'd been working on. All the mortar surrounding it had now been removed – at least the mortar on *his* side of the wall. He tried pushing at it, but it wouldn't budge. There was still enough mortar beyond the point he could dig to keep the brick solidly in place. He pushed again, and the pushing made his already-tender hand sore. He guessed he must have been pushing at the brick before he'd fallen asleep.

Still Lady Arbella wept, and Richard felt very helpless and frustrated. If he couldn't break through this wall, then what was the point of anything? After five days of almost continual excavating, it had become the sole purpose of his life. Yet what if he couldn't do it? What if he ended up breaking the bones of his hands on a brick that would never yield?

He couldn't allow such doubts to take him over, or else his mind would start to crumble. He had to keep trying. This time he leaned back against the leg of his bed for support, applying the whole weight of his body behind his arm and shoulder. He would *not* let the brick defeat him. As he pushed, a surge of furious energy shot through his veins, and he growled deep down in his chest. The veins in his head bulged, the skin on his palm burned and his bones screamed as if about to shatter, but he didn't care. He imagined himself as no longer flesh but oak: a battering ram. *I have to do this... There is nothing else...*

Then something shifted beneath his hand.

It was a very small shift, but he'd definitely felt it. His dry lips parted in a smile. After a pause to catch his breath, he pushed again, this time with added confidence. A deep grinding sound came from within the wall, and Richard let out a strangled cheer as the brick started to slide backwards. Once the last of the mortar had broken away, the brick moved freely.

He kept pushing it until it fell out of the back of the wall. A faint *clink* followed as it hit the ground on the far side. Peering through the gap in the brickwork, he could see nothing but pure darkness. This was disappointing. What had he hoped for? A view directly into Lady Arbella's bedchamber? He should have known not to expect that. Walls in a house such as this were unlikely to be one brick-width thick. What he'd found was a mysterious hollow area between his wall and hers.

Arbella had stopped crying by now. Perhaps she had become alarmed by the noises coming from behind her own hearth and was now cowering on the far side of the room. Ought he to risk calling out to her? But what if a guard heard him? Or what if she called to a guard for help, thinking he wished her ill?

As he was sitting there pondering what to do, he heard a muted scuffling sound on the other side of the wall. Something was climbing up out of the blackness. Richard fell backwards in surprise as a small, grey, furry head poked its nose out of the gap between the bricks. It stared at him with glossy black eyes that seemed both indignant and suspicious. After wrinkling its nose at Richard, the rat squeezed its plump body through the narrow opening and flopped down onto the floor, then quickly scuttled under his bed. Richard wasn't disgusted by the sight, being well used to living at close quarters with rodents in the forest – but it did get him thinking. If a rat could live behind that wall, then it couldn't be a completely closed-off space. Of course the rat could have found its way in there through tiny cracks or outflow pipes from the building's outer wall. Or perhaps it found a means of access from Lady Arbella's side. He hoped that was the case.

Richard put his eye close to the opening, straining to see the faintest chink of light in the darkness, but there was nothing. He couldn't hear anything either – no more ratlike scufflings, and nothing from Lady Arbella. He tried to imagine what she must be thinking. She'd be scared, obviously. Her first thought would be that the sounds he was making represented danger. If he made any more noise now, her most likely response would be to summon a guard. It was therefore vital to reassure her that he meant no harm. He moved his mouth very close to the opening and curved his hands around his mouth so that his voice would be directed towards her room and away from the guards outside. Then, in a hoarse whisper, he called: 'Lady Arbella!'

Silence.

'Lady Arbella, I'm a prisoner like you. I'm in the room next door.'

He waited, but heard nothing...

'I'm a friend,' he said. 'I want to help you... Please say something so I know you can hear me.'

Richard waited tensely for a moment, alert to the smallest sound.

Eventually, he tried again: 'Lady Arbella.'

As he said this, her voice cut in, startlingly close:

'Who are you?' she hissed.

He shuddered. *She'd heard him! They were communicating!*

'My name is Richard Fletcher,' he said more softly now – for he now knew she was close enough to hear him clearly. 'I was captured by Sir Griffin, and brought here. I've been kept in this room for ten days.'

'How are we speaking?' she asked.

'There's a hollow space in the wall between our rooms.'

'And how do you plan to help me… Richard Fletcher?'

It gave him goosebumps to hear her say his name. He had fantasized about this moment on so many occasions while digging with his nail.

'How do you plan to help me?' she asked again.

And then it struck him, with a sagging feeling inside, that he didn't have any idea how he was going to help her.

'I want to help you escape, my lady,' he said, trying to sound more certain than he felt. 'We can work together to find a way out of here.'

'Do you have a plan, sir?'

'Not yet,' he admitted – then bit his lip, wishing he hadn't said that. This conversation wasn't proceeding as he'd played it out in his head. He needed to sound more sure of himself, more heroic. 'I am confident,' he said, 'that I will find us a means of escape.'

'I don't believe you will be able to help me, sir,' she said bleakly. 'You are the second to have tried, and like the other fellow, you seem doomed to fail.'

By 'the other fellow' Richard assumed she meant

the young man who had come to his door a week ago.

'We are surrounded by water, and by guards,' she continued. 'There is nothing we can do but be resigned to our fate.'

This was depressing to hear. Did he inspire so little confidence in her? Feeling rather dispirited, he lapsed into silence.

'Are you still there?' she asked after a few moments.

'Aye.'

'You have a pleasing voice,' she said.

'Thank you, my lady.'

'There is a strength in you.'

Richard allowed himself a modest smile.

'Is it possible for me to see you?' she asked.

'To… see me?'

'One cannot judge a man by his voice alone,' she said. 'See if you can find a way into this room so I can look upon your face. That way I will know if you are someone in whom I can place my trust.'

'My lady…'

'Think of it as a test. If you can find your way in here, then perhaps you are clever enough to discover a way out of this castle.'

'I will do my utmost,' said Richard, feeling much more encouraged. 'If there is a way to you, rest assured I shall find it. Prithee, wait there for me.'

This elicited a small laugh from the other side of the wall. It was the first time he'd heard her express amusement or any pleasurable emotion, and it stunned him. Why had she laughed?

'Of course I shall be waiting here for you, sir,' she said, with the same musical laughter in her voice. 'Where else would I go?'

Now he wanted to laugh at himself for being so foolish. Still, he didn't regret it, for he was enraptured by the thought that something he'd said had amused her – even if he hadn't meant it to. It delighted him to picture her kneeling there smiling on the other side of the wall.

Nervously, he pushed his hand and then his arm through the slot created by the missing brick. He reached into the darkness as far as he could, until his upper arm became too bulky to pass through the gap. Yet even with his arm, hand and fingers fully extended, he couldn't reach Lady Arbella's wall. The space between the walls was bigger than he'd imagined. It was capacious enough for a human to sit comfortably in, let alone a rat. Why would such a space be constructed? Perhaps it was a place for someone to hide in. That would explain the false hearth...

And then he remembered that this was a house where Catholics lived – a house that priests might sometimes visit to celebrate mass. And if a priest happened to be here when the authorities came calling, he would need somewhere to hide. This could be one of those places. But if this was a hiding-place for a priest, it followed that there must be some means of getting into it – other than painstakingly digging out each brick. Perhaps it could only be accessed from Lady Arbella's side.

Richard stretched and stretched some more, squeezing his upper arm further into the gap until he almost feared getting himself stuck there. Yet however far he stretched, he couldn't reach the far wall. He did, however, feel a weak draft against his hand, so there *was* a flow of air – more evidence that this was a place where a man could hide out for a prolonged period. He tried bending his arm and investigating the remainder of the space, to see if there were walls within reach to the right or left. He found none. The hollow was becoming increasingly spacious in his mind's eye.

As his hand neared the back of his own hearth wall, he felt something surprising. It was a thick, vertical bar – cold and hard to the touch, like iron. He tried to move it, but couldn't, so he guessed it was fixed to the wall. He gripped it and tried pulling it again, this time towards him. To his great surprise, this effort gave rise to a deep rumbling sound, and the iron bar, together with the entire wall, slid several inches to the right.

Chapter 28

Lady Arbella's Plan

Richard gasped to see the black interior of the hollow space thus exposed. The wall that had seemed so solid and unmoveable – the wall that he'd been painstakingly picking at for five solid days – was now revealed to be a sliding door. Did this mean he could simply have pulled it sideways on day one, and it would have opened? If so, he wanted to cry for all the wasted time and effort. Grimacing with pain and frustration, he yanked out his arm and put his hands to the exposed side of the wall to push it further open. It moved surprisingly – depressingly – smoothly. Aye, he was a fool if ever there was one! But perhaps it would be better if he didn't mention any of this to Lady Arbella, or it might just dash any hope he had of winning her confidence.

He crawled into the tiny, dark, brick-lined chamber. It was about six feet long and three feet deep. The floor was thick with dust and rat droppings, and there was a low, vaulted ceiling an inch or so above his bowed head. This would not have been a comfortable place to hide for more than a few hours. The wall opposite – the back of Lady Arbella's hearth, he presumed – also had a vertical iron bar fixed to it. He grasped hold of this and tugged it in a sideways direction. It seemed, at first, to be jammed, but after a second, firmer yank, it slid sharply rightwards. Light flooded in, and he heard a gasp of surprise. He could see, through the gap, the corner of a bed, a wash-stand, a chest and a mirror. After sliding it further, he saw, near the bed, the hem of a long dress.

Richard wriggled out of the hiding-place and climbed awkwardly to his feet. Brushing the dust from his shoulders, he kept his head bowed. He found it barely possible to set his eyes upon the lady who had occupied his thoughts so intensely these past ten days.

'Look at me,' she commanded. And he did so.

Lady Arbella was small and delicate and beautiful – like a woodland bird, thought Richard, a goldcrest or a jay, that fluttered into the sky before you could get close to it. She had fragile blue eyes, a small pink mouth and smooth, very pale, aristocratic skin. He half expected her to vanish under his crude gaze, like a vision or dream – nothing so exquisite could be real.

'That is enough,' she said. 'Your stare is becoming tiresome.'

Richard flicked his eyes back down to the rug on the floor. 'Please forgive me, ma'am,' he mumbled.

'You did well, Richard.' She was speaking more gently now. 'You found your way in here sooner than expected.' He felt her scrutiny, and his cheeks grew hot. 'What is more,' she said, 'you have a nice face. It is a face I believe I can trust. You are, perhaps, a little young. But one has to make allowances. So if you remain willing to help me, then I am prepared to entrust you with the task we spoke of.'

'The task…?'

'Aye, the task of conveying me safely from this place and restoring me to my home.'

Richard didn't remember phrasing it quite like that. All the same, he was overjoyed at being granted such a mission. He bowed to her. 'My lady, I am honoured. I will not let you down.'

She glanced at the door. 'We do not have long. The guard will bring in my meal soon. I must tell you my plan.'

'You have a plan?' Richard was astonished.

'Of course I have a plan. Do you think a woman cannot plot or scheme as well as men can? I concocted the plan while I was waiting for you. But before I tell you it, I want you to tell me why you are here. Why did they capture you?'

Richard shrugged. 'They wish me to kill someone.'

She drew back from him, her lips trembling.

'*K-Kill* someone? What kind of a man are you?'

'Not a killer,' said Richard quickly. 'I'm an archer, a hunter from the forest.'

'Whom do they wish you to kill?'

He ground his teeth, recalling the wooden target with the crown. He didn't want to tell her of his suspicions. He felt shamed by them.

'We have no time for guessing games, Mr Fletcher. Who is it?'

'The king,' said Richard.

Arbella closed her eyes. When she opened them again, her expression was one of grim sorrow. 'It is as I feared,' she said. 'Sir Griffin told me he had brought me here for my own safety – that supporters of King James wanted to kill me because I was a threat to his rule. I knew that couldn't be true. I feared – and now you have confirmed – that the threat is not out there. It's right here. Sir Griffin and his friends mean to kill King James and place me on the throne in his stead.'

Richard's jaw dropped open. 'You... Queen of England?'

She nodded and sighed, slumping miserably on her bed. 'I am the king's cousin, the great granddaughter of King Henry VII. It is my curse, Richard, to be related to such men. All I have ever desired was a quiet life, to live modestly, to marry the man I love.'

Richard swallowed. 'And you shall, my lady, have all of that. You have my word.' This was what he'd wanted, what he'd planned for, so why did it hurt him so much inside to promise it?

She smiled sadly and wiped away a tear as she stared up towards the canopy of her bed. 'Not all of that is within your gift, young man. But I thank you even so.' Lowering her gaze to him, she said: 'You are *so* innocent. Perhaps you have spent too much time in the forest and not enough in human society. But what you lack in experience, you make up for in kindness. You are a sweet, simple soul, and these people are cruel to try and turn you into a murderer.'

'I won't let them,' vowed Richard. 'I won't kill the king for anything.'

'Nay, you won't,' said Arbella. 'But you'll show willing, won't you?'

'Forgive me, ma'am. I don't unders…'

'That is my plan, Richard,' she said, '– for both of us… We will pretend to accept the roles assigned to us. You will agree to kill the king, and I will agree to be their puppet queen. We will lull them into believing that we are their creatures. And then, when their plans reach fruition and they finally take us out of this moated castle, you will make your move, and free us both.'

'I'll make my move,' repeated Richard. He could picture it now – a coach hurtling along a forest road, he and Lady Arbella seated within. With his hunting reflexes, he'd dive upon the guards, seize the reins from the driver. In just a few beats of his Lady's heart, he'd be in control, carrying her to freedom – to the quiet life she cherished.

He would do this for her, even if he died trying.

She broke into his thoughts with a question: 'What was your life before the forest, Richard?'

'I remember very little of it,' he murmured. 'Though lately I've been troubled by dreams of a girl. I think she was dear to me once.'

Arbella smiled. 'Your true love?'

'Nay. Though I loved her very much. I believe I would have done anything for her. And yet I did not desire her in the way one would a lover.'

'Your sister then?'

Richard brightened at this. Of course! He nodded delightedly. 'She was my sister!'

Arbella frowned through her smile. 'It is quite strange that you do not remember having a sister.'

'That life was stolen from me – my memories, too, save for these dreams. Now I am endeavouring to forget it.'

'Wouldn't you like to find your sister again?'

'Aye, of course, but there's little chance of that. We lived in London, I believe – a city of two hundred thousand souls. How would I ever find her?'

He felt the touch of Arbella's hand on his arm, and it sent tremors through his skin. 'You must have hope, Richard,' she said. 'You vowed to help me. And I vow, in return, to do whatever I can to help you find your sister.'

'Thank you, my lady.'

They heard a creak in the passageway outside.

A guard had arrived.

'They're bringing my meal,' hissed Arbella. 'Quick, back to your room!'

Richard could hear the key turning in the lock of her door as he scrambled back through her hearth and heaved it shut behind him. Then he hauled himself out of the dark hole and into his own room before tugging his hearth wall closed. He leaned against it and waited for his heart to become calm again.

He began to reflect upon his encounter with Lady Arbella – her startling beauty and refinement, her vulnerability. What did she think of him? She called him innocent and simple, and yet she seemed to like and trust him. As he was recalling these things, he heard a squeak near his foot. The rat had emerged from under the bed and was studying his shoe.

'Good day to you, little friend,' said Richard. The rat wrinkled its nose at him. 'Did you know, I've just met a woman who could be the next queen of England. She's a cousin of the king, so very high born.'

The rat sniffed at his shoe. Richard barely noticed. His eyes became dreamy. 'I fancy she liked me a little. She said I had a nice face.' His heart beat harder as he recalled her voice saying those words. Then he drew back from the thought, reminding himself that nothing could ever happen between them. They were worlds apart, he and Arbella. 'I have as much chance of winning her heart as you have of marrying a beautiful white mouse,' he said to the rat. 'Still, she promised to help me find this girl I'm always dreaming about. This sister I never knew I had. Can you believe that, Rat? A sister!

'I wonder where she is...'

Chapter 29

The Uses of Love

Alice lay on a straw mattress on the dungeon floor. Her eyes were closed. She appeared to be asleep. She *wanted* to be asleep, yet she remained awake – alive to the pain in her arms, legs and back. It came in waves, crisping and crackling on her skin like fire. The guards had beaten her so many times, laying welts upon welts, bruises upon bruises. Pointy Beard, whose name she now knew to be Catesby, had stood nearby and watched the whole thing, firing questions at her between the blows.

But after three days of torture, she hadn't told him anything – anything important, at least. As far as he knew, she was a player with the King's Men, a friend of Will Shakespeare's, who had come here to rescue him. But Will hadn't wanted to be rescued. He'd left her in search of the library to research his new play – and he'd found a female prisoner instead. Alice had gone to her because she thought they might be able to help each other escape from the castle. She didn't know who the lady was, and had never seen or heard of her before she walked into her room.

This was the story she kept on repeating and repeating, no matter how hard or often they beat her. She had tried to stay as close to the truth as she could, hoping it would align with Will's version of events – because Catesby must have questioned him, too. The last thing she wanted was to get Will in trouble. He hadn't asked for any of this.

There was one secret Alice had been forced to reveal, and that was her gender. Catesby had ripped her shirt from her back before the first beating, and he'd seen the cloth she'd wound around her chest.

'So, you're a girl!' he declared in a triumphant tone. 'Why were you pretending to be a boy?'

'Why do you think?' Alice snapped back. 'I'm a player. Girls can't be players.'

'Nor spies,' he laughed. 'What's your name then?'

'Eve,' she replied, happy to give him that. It was what Gus Phillips called her when they were alone and he felt like taunting her – Gus and Tom were the only other living people who knew her secret.

Catesby was delighted by the name. He threw back his head and laughed. 'So, Eve,' he said. 'Now I know your name and your gender. The rest shouldn't be too difficult to extract. Tell me the real reason why you're here. Who are you working for?'

But Alice hadn't told him – she'd sooner bite her tongue off than do that. Instead, she just repeated the same story. And the beatings had continued.

The door to the dungeon squeaked open and Catesby entered. She knew his soft, deliberate tread even without opening her eyes. It made her whole body want to curl up and crawl into a crack in the floor. His footsteps approached her bed, and she heard the rustle of his clothing as he kneeled down beside her, then smelled his warm, stale, beery breath as he leaned close. She managed not to flinch, wanting him to believe she was asleep.

'Are you ready to talk yet, Eve?' he murmured. 'Because I'm ready to listen.'

'Maybe she is what she says she is,' said another voice, a little further off. It was Markham. He had a gentler temperament than Catesby, and Alice was always relieved when he was around – she also dreaded when he left, because a beating usually followed.

'Quiet!' hissed Catesby. 'Don't let her hear you entertain such thoughts.'

'She's asleep,' said Markham. 'Probably exhausted, poor thing. Can't you just accept that she might be a player who came to rescue her friend, then accidentally wandered into the wrong room?'

Catesby sighed. 'You remember that fiasco at the Globe, during the Essex rebellion?'

'Aye.'

'The day after, as we were preparing to march on the City, Sir Gelly told me something. He said there was a boy there at the Globe, one of the Chamberlain's Men as they were known then. During the fight on the balcony, this boy suddenly flew down from the roof of the playhouse and knocked over Edmund Squires. Sir Gelly thought the lad might have been working for the Beagle. He had no proof, just a hunch.'

'You think Eve might have been the "boy"?'

Listening to this, Alice scarcely dared breathe. She tried to keep her face impassive.

'Maybe – who knows?' answered Catesby. 'But players and spies, they're not so different, are they? Artful, devious types, adept at playing parts – especially this one, hiding the fact that she's a girl. I wouldn't put it past the Beagle to have planted her as a spy within the King's Men.'

The door opened once more, and a guard entered.

'Sir, Father William Watson has arrived.'

Alice stiffened. *Watson? Here? How did he get out of prison? This was a disaster! If he saw her, they'd all know for sure that she was working for Cecil...*

Markham sounded equally taken aback by this news. 'Father Watson? Then he must have broken out of the Clink...'

'Let's hope he wasn't followed,' muttered Catesby, rising to his feet.

'Show him into the great hall,' Markham said to the

guard. 'We'll be with him shortly.'

Alice let out a relieved breath. At least the terrifying priest wouldn't be coming into the dungeon. She prayed it would be a brief visit and he'd be on his way soon.

But then she heard a deep voice echoing in the stairwell: 'Out of my way, scoundrel! You won't show me into anywhere, Markham. I'm coming to you now!'

Alice cringed. She tried desperately to crawl into the shadows, every movement causing excruciating pain in the bruised parts of her back and legs. Through half-closed eyelids, she glimpsed a guard getting flung aside as a ferocious-looking Father Watson burst into the dungeon. There was mud on his boots and breeches and his red face glowed like fire reflected in wet leather. His cropped grey hair stuck up from his scalp as if he'd been struck by lightning.

'I've been riding non-stop for sixteen hours,' he growled at Markham, 'and I won't be shown anywhere, you swine.

'Forgive me, Father,' cowered Markham.

'I have news,' thundered Watson. 'Grievous news. And it cannot wait.'

'What news?' asked Catesby.

Watson noticed him for the first time, and frowned. 'Catesby, you old snake. I'm glad to find you here. The authorities have got wind of our plans. They know we're at Bradenstoke.'

'*But how?*' cried Markham.

'That young messenger I sent you – the one calling himself Tom. He had me fooled with his recusant act. Turned out he was one of the Beagle's agents.'

'No!' wailed Markham.

Desperate fears flooded Alice's heart. *What did he do to Tom when he found out who he was?* A brute like Watson wouldn't have hesitated to kill him, and in a savage fashion.

'I take it you slaughtered the villainous little canker-blossom for his treachery, Father?' said Catesby.

'I did not. He turned out to be more useful to me alive.'

Alice silently shuddered with relief.

'How so?' asked Catesby.

'I've made him my creature – turned him against his masters. I made him tell them you've moved the prisoners to Hesleyside Hall in Northumberland. It should buy us some time, though not much.'

'How did you turn him, Father?' asked Markham. 'Was it through the power of the Lord?'

'Nay, it's a different kind of power he's in the grip of – *love*. There's a young man he's besotted with, a player with the King's Men. I made him believe we'd captured the youth and were holding him prisoner here. I said we'd kill him if he didn't do as I said.'

Alice was left shocked and somewhat lightheaded by this revelation. Tom… *loved her?* Questions began bursting like sparks in her head. Could it really be true? And how could Watson know about it if it was? Why would Tom confide his feelings to him of all people?

Her mind flashed back to that moment behind the Anchor tavern when they'd stood so close and she'd felt a mysterious pull between them, and that bittersweet ache as she left him. Had he felt that too, or something like it?

But whatever that feeling was, it was being ruthlessly exploited by Watson, and now it placed her in grave danger. For Catesby and Markham must have made the connection. The silence from the pair of them following Watson's announcement filled her with foreboding. Alice could imagine them exchanging amused glances.

'Have you met this youth, Father?' asked Catesby in a voice thick with dark mirth.

Alice tensed, waiting for the inevitable.

'Aye,' Watson answered. 'He, too, attempted to pass himself off as a recusant at the Clink, but I saw through him right away.'

'Come this way,' Catesby invited him. 'I have someone to show you.'

Fear turned her rigid. She tried to maintain her pretence of sleep, finding what refuge she could behind the thin shield of her eyelids.

Three sets of footsteps rasped on the stone-slabbed floor, closing in on her supine form. When they stopped, Father Watson exclaimed 'That's him!', and he uttered a raucous laugh. 'By all the saints, what were the chances? You have the very one! And I see you've given him a beating.'

'*Him* is a *her*,' said Catesby. 'We found that out in the course of the beating.'

'These players, eh?' muttered Watson. 'The many masks they wear... Still, it makes no difference what she is, boy or girl. Her value lies in the affection she arouses in our double agent. What induced you to seize her?'

'We didn't,' said Catesby. 'She came here of her own volition, soon after we captured Shakespeare. She claimed her sole purpose was to rescue the playwright, yet we found her in Lady Arbella's chamber. It seems I was right to be suspicious.'

'Aye, she's as much a spy as her lover boy. She came here to snatch Arbella alright.'

'It would be my greatest pleasure to run her through with my sword right now,' said Catesby.

'And mine,' growled Watson.

Alice heard the hiss of a sword being unsheathed, and she trembled, waiting for the final, excruciating pain as the blade sliced into her. She tried to prepare herself mentally for death – *the undiscovered country*, as Will called it. But her mind was confusion: too many tumbling thoughts, too many regrets. *Richard... Tom...*

Then Markham said: 'Wouldn't it be best if we kept her alive for now? We can use her to keep Tom loyal.'

'Aye, I suppose you're right,' sighed Watson, sheathing his sword.

Alice took a tiny breath – hardly daring to believe she'd escaped.

'Let's take her with us when we leave tonight,' said Watson.

'*Tonight?*' cried Markham. 'But it'll take me at least a week to pack everything up.'

'We don't have that sort of time,' said Watson. 'This place will be swarming with soldiers by tomorrow. The bulk of Cecil's forces may be heading to Northumberland, but he'll almost certainly send a local detachment here to search for clues. Take nothing but the bare essentials – and the prisoners, of course. We must be on the road by midnight.'

Markham grunted. 'I'll do my best… But where are we going?'

'Anywhere but here or Hesleyside,' said Watson. 'Have you two not got friends or family in the vicinity who you can trust to be discreet?'

'We'll go to Coughton Court, the home of my cousin Bess Throckmorton,' said Catesby. 'It's about ten miles south-west of here. Bess is a recusant. She can be trusted.'

'Very good,' said Watson.

The three then departed the dungeon, along with the guards.

Once she knew she was alone, Alice stretched her aching body and tried to find a more comfortable position. How quickly fortunes could change. Moments earlier, she was on the brink of a horrid and pitiful death. Now, she felt the first stirrings of renewed hope. Tom must have worked out the conspirators were abandoning Bradenstoke. He would be on his way here now. If he could only arrive before they left, there was a chance he could effect a rescue – or at least provide enough of a distraction to allow her to escape. If only she didn't feel so weak...

Chapter 30

kill on Sight

BRADENSTOKE HALL, 13TH MAY 1603

When Tom arrived at Bradenstoke in the early hours of the morning, the gates stood eerily open. The moon, rising above the tree line, shone a cool, unfriendly gleam upon the surface of the moat. No lamps burned in the windows. This was inauspicious. The castle appeared undefended, maybe even deserted. Had they already abandoned it? Or was this a trap? Uneasily, he coaxed Gunpowder through the gates. The horse snorted spurts of steam from its nostrils as it trotted across the bridge, hoofbeats echoing. Approaching the gatehouse, Tom was met by the porter, who raised his halberd and shouted: 'Who goes there?'

'A friend,' replied Tom, showing him his fish scar.

The porter glowered at it a moment, then waved him through.

'Is Sir Griffin here?' Tom asked him.

'I don't know,' grumbled the porter, scratching his belly. 'I've just come on duty. If he is, he'll be a-bed by now, along with the servants, so there's no one around to fix you up with a room for the night. You can bed down in the stables until morning if you want.'

Tom thanked him and advanced into the courtyard. He remembered how pleasant and welcoming it had appeared on his first visit. Tonight, it seemed a pale shadow of itself – barely solid, like a crudely formed model. He dismounted and tethered Gunpowder to a pillar, then mounted a set of steps and pushed open the unbolted main door. The interior was cold and dark. Glancing around, he spotted a lamp glow emanating from a room to the left of the great hall. The door was ajar and he could hear voices from within – one deep, the other with a boyish pitch. He recognised the latter as belonging to Roland, the young groom he'd met last time. Tom strode towards the door, intending to announce himself – but then he stopped as he caught a mention of his name.

'Tom Cavendish he calls himself,' Roland was saying. 'He bears the sign of the fish, but Sir Griffin says he's turned traitor…'

'Why are *you* telling me this?' demanded the deeper voice. 'As head guard, I normally take my orders directly from Sir Griffin.'

'Sir Griffin is gone, Joseph. He left some hours ago, together with Mr Catesby and the other prisoners.'

When he heard this, Tom gritted his teeth in frustration. As he'd suspected, he was too late. *But where did they go?*

'Where did they go?' asked Joseph, as if he'd become the mouthpiece for Tom's thoughts.

'That's none of your concern,' retorted Roland. 'Your duty is to make sure this character, Tom Cavendish, is killed upon arrival…'

Killed? Tom's heart jolted. He had to get away the castle, and fast – but not before he'd discovered where Alice and the others had been taken.

'And he *will* arrive, most likely tonight,' Roland continued. 'Here, this is a rough sketch of his face. Go and show it to the other guards. And remember: he's to be killed on sight.'

'Very good, master Roland,' replied Joseph, a little begrudgingly.

Hearing Joseph's footsteps approaching the door, Tom stepped smartly into the shadows behind it. As he backed closer to the wall, something sharp poked him in the back, making him gasp. Glancing behind, he discovered he'd nearly impaled himself on a ceremonial weapon displayed on the wall.

Joseph emerged from the room, passing mere inches from Tom as he strode towards the door leading to the courtyard. Very soon, he'd show the sketch to the porter, the alarm would be raised, and Tom would be trapped. He had to act fast. The weapon he'd hurt himself on turned out to be a heavy, club-like mace. He lifted it from its hook. The weapon was heavy, and weighed him down as he lumbered across the lobby.

He found Joseph standing at the top of the steps, staring at Gunpowder. Tom could almost see the cogs working in the head guard's brain: an unfamiliar horse; perhaps Tom Cavendish had already arrived. Joseph took a breath, as if about to cry out an alarm. Straining under the weight, Tom heaved the mace up to shoulder height and swung it, striking Joseph on the back of the head. The man emitted a muted grunt, his legs collapsed beneath him and he toppled quietly down the steps, landing in an unconscious heap. Tom quickly ran down and dragged him into the shadows at the side of the steps before anyone saw him. He flung the weapon down next to him.

It was then that Tom spotted the paper Joseph had been carrying – the paper containing the sketch of Tom's face. Joseph had dropped it when he'd been hit, and it had landed on the cobbles a few feet from the steps. As Tom sneaked out and tried to grab it, a breeze lifted up the paper and caused it to flutter across the courtyard. Tom began to chase after it.

At that moment, a guard emerged into the courtyard from a doorway on the left. The guard saw what was happening, and decided to help Tom by chasing after it himself. Tom put on a spurt of speed, desperate to reach it before the guard could see what was on it. He managed – just. But as he reached for the paper, it blew away again, straight into the guard's outstretched hand.

'Yours, I presume,' said the guard, handing it to him.

'Aye,' said Tom breathlessly, rolling it up tightly and stuffing it into his pocket. 'It's a–a message for Sir Griffin.' He showed him his fish scar.

The guard recognised it and stood a little more erect. 'Sir Griffin's not here,' he said. 'He left just after midnight.'

'Where did he go?' asked Tom, not really expecting the man to know.

'Coughton Court. It's about ten miles from here. Take the main road through the forest, and when it forks, head south.'

'Thank you!' gushed Tom, hastening to untether his horse. His fingers felt clumsy as he struggled to unknot the rope. Out of the corner of his eye, he could already see Joseph by the steps beginning to stir.

Suddenly, a small figure rushed out of the house. It was Roland. The boy's face was alive with bloodthirsty rage.

Pointing at Tom, he screamed: 'Kill him!'

Tom ripped the rope from the pillar and leapt

astride Gunpowder. He spurred it into a gallop across the courtyard just as Joseph, with one hand clamped to the back of his head, leapt up and lunged at the reins.

Joseph missed, and Tom accelerated, kicking at the other guard as he tried to grab his foot. The guard clung onto Tom's ankle and was dragged along in his wake, his knees bumping along the cobbles. Tom clung on, but the guard's weight was slowing him down and threatened to pull him right off his horse.

Meanwhile, the porter must have rushed up inside the gatehouse, for now the portcullis was descending. Tom, still some twenty yards from the gatehouse, could see that the spikes had almost reached the height of his head and were getting lower all the time. In desperation, he reached down and pulled at the guard's fingers, still grimly clinging on. He forced the middle finger back to breaking point. The man screamed and finally released his grip.

Tom now urged Gunpowder forward, but he feared he was too late: the portcullis looked extremely low. He ducked his head right down, so his nose was touching the pommel of his saddle. Squeezing his eyes shut, he prayed. An iron spike brushed the back of his head as he flashed beneath the portcullis. Behind him, Roland uttered a despairing scream. Racing across the bridge, Tom could smell the damp, fresh forest ahead, and his heart surged.

Chapter 31

In a Few Beats of His Lady's Heart

THE FOREST OF ARDEN, 13TH MAY 1603

The coach, pulled by four horses, moved at speed along the dark forest road. Richard had a sack over his head and a rope tied around his neck to hold it in place. Another rope bound his wrists behind his back. The carriage rattled and swayed along the potholed track, rocking Richard and his fellow passengers from side to side. They bashed against each other and bounced off the coach's cushioned leather walls, and the clatter of the wheels and the squeals of the wood-and-iron undercarriage were so loud as to make conversation impossible.

Richard had been elated earlier when Markham informed him they were leaving Bradenstoke. This was the chance he and Lady Arbella had hoped for to stage an escape, and it had come far sooner than they'd expected – only a matter of hours after they'd made their plans. But the situation he now found himself in was a long way from the one he had envisaged earlier in her room. What chance did he have, trussed up like this, to dive upon the guard or seize the drivers' reins? He couldn't even use his hunter's eyes to watch for opportunities, stuck inside this dark, smelly sack.

An hour earlier, he'd been escorted from his room at Bradenstoke to the stables, where the guards had placed the sack over his head and bound his wrists. After unceremoniously pushing him into the coach, a guard climbed in and took the seat diagonally opposite. A short while later, Markham joined them – Richard recognised him from his voice. With him was someone else, who occupied the coach's fourth and final seat. Markham had asked 'Are you comfortable, my lady?', and she had replied briefly that she was.

Richard had experienced a warm thrill at the sound of Arbella's voice – strained and miserable though it may have been. She was here, just inches away, on the bench opposite, their knees almost touching. He fancied occasionally, as they clattered through the night, that he could hear her breathe or shift in her seat – but it was hard to be sure amid all the noise. Her proximity gave him hope, yet also reinforced his sense of failure. For here he was, sitting so close to the lady he had resolved to rescue, and powerless to make any progress towards that goal.

Richard had spent the whole journey straining at the rope that bound his wrists behind his back, trying to stretch it enough to be able to squeeze his hands through. But it was hopeless. The rope was thick and the knot tight. The skin of his wrists burned from all the chafing and pulling, yet the rope felt as tight as ever. Time, he guessed, was against them, to judge from the speed at which they were travelling. No team of horses could maintain such a pace for any length of time, which meant the journey had to be short. Soon they would arrive at their destination and be locked away once again in guarded rooms, the opportunity for escape gone.

Richard was pondering the cruelty of fate when the coach was suddenly shaken by a violent bump. One of the wheels had hit a deep rut. He was thrown back in his seat and at the same time felt someone fall heavily against him. He heard her gentle, embarrassed gasp. For less than a second, he felt Arbella's small, slender body against his, and caught her sweet, heady scent. Then, abruptly, she moved away, no doubt jerked back into her seat by the guard sitting next to her.

Richard closed his eyes, his senses reeling. As the carriage resumed its bumpy rhythm, he leaned back – and encountered something on the seat behind him, something that hadn't been there before. It was small and metallic. With his fingers, he traced the edge of a blade.

A knife!

Where had it come from?

And then he understood... Lady Arbella had placed it there, behind his back, when she had fallen against him. She must have been waiting for such an opportunity. How resourceful of her! Now he would be able to cut through the rope. He grasped the knife's handle with his fingers and embedded it as deep as he could into the tight space between the seat and the seat back. This secured it. Between thumb and forefinger, he carefully rotated the blade so one of its sharp sides was pointing outwards, close to his wrists. Now he began running the rope back and forth along the edge of the blade. The jolting of the coach helped, as he could use that motion to work the rope against the sharp edge without attracting attention. Soon, he could feel the rope start to fray and loosen, and he sensed the pressure of the blade cutting ever closer to his skin.

It was working, but not quickly enough. Richard was haunted by the thought that at any moment the coach would arrive at its destination. He redoubled his efforts, forcing the rope ever more violently on the little knife. He felt a painful slash near his thumb as he accidentally moved his hand too close to the blade. But he didn't relent, and the rope kept thinning until it was only a few strands thick. After a final burst of pressure, it broke.

Richard felt elated. His hands were now free, ready to spring a surprise. Yet he was careful to maintain the same posture with his shoulders forced back and his wrists pushed tightly together, as if nothing had changed. With his fingers he deftly drew the knife out of the seat and took a firm grip of its handle. He would have to act fast and decisively. Failure would mean instant death. Markham and Catesby may once have valued him as their assassin, but his defiant attitude had seen his status plummet. Without question, the guard would be under orders to kill him if he tried to escape. The guard would therefore have to be dealt with first.

Richard used to do a breathing trick, trying to achieve a balance between calmness and tension while crouched on a low tree branch poised to ambush forest animals. Now he used the same technique, taking slow, deep breaths to calm his heart as he rehearsed each stage of his plan in his head. He had already mentally mapped the interior layout of the coach and the position of its passengers, even though he'd never seen any of it. Seated to his left was Markham. Directly opposite was Lady Arbella, and the guard was diagonally opposite on his left. The door was on his right, the handle on Arbella's side. He knew what needed to be done. Now all that remained was to do it.

After taking a final breath, Richard sprang into action.

Chapter 32

A Spark of Dread and Wild Excitement

Richard lurched diagonally towards the guard, bringing his right arm around and driving the knife into what he hoped was the man's shoulder – for he had no desire to kill him. The guard emitted a gurgling roar. Keeping the knife pressed there, Richard raised his left arm and swung it, elbow first, into Markham's face. He struck something hard and knobbly that may have been his cheek or nose. Markham grunted, and Richard hit him again, this time using his fist like a hammer. He heard a small crack.

The guard's hand, meanwhile, was flailing near Richard's face, and now it grabbed his throat, just above the encircling rope, and squeezed, in an attempt to throttle him. Richard retaliated by exerting more pressure on the knife and twisting it. The guard let out another strangled scream and his hand fell away. With nothing but pitiful moans now coming from both men, Richard pulled the knife free of the guard and quickly unloosed the rope from around his neck before ripping the sack off his head.

Squinting through the gloom, he quickly appraised the situation. His aim had been good. The guard was sprawled in his seat, blood soaking his left shoulder. Markham was bent forward almost to his knees, hand covering his broken nose. Richard had bought himself seconds, no more than that.

Lady Arbella, ghostly pale, was sitting tense and still in her corner of the carriage. Yet there was an impressive calmness in the set of her lips.

'My lady,' said Richard, 'I must stop this carriage, so we can alight. Prithee, wait here for me.'

'Of course I shall, sir,' she murmured. 'Where else would I go?'

Was that the faintest hint of a smile upon her face?

They won't harm her, he told himself as he pushed open the door and stepped into the rushing wind and the night. She is their jewel as much as she is mine. Without her, they, like me, are nothing…

He edged along the running board towards the

thundering black horses, his hands struggling to find a purchase on the coach's waxen cerecloth and leather exterior. Reaching the front, he grabbed hold of the iron frame at the base of the driver's seat, just inches from the juddering, spinning wheel. The wind blasted at his face. Mud whipping in from the wheel spattered his tunic. Raising his head, he glimpsed the driver with his long whip framed against the moon. The man was oblivious to his presence – but wouldn't be for long. With the agility of a practised tree climber, Richard clambered up the iron frame until he was crouched behind the driver. Then he shoved him hard. The driver gave a brief yell as he fell into the road and tumbled into the ditch. Richard had no time to worry about the poor fellow's fate. He grabbed the reins just before they fell out of reach between the horses, and pulled on them as hard as he could. The horses neighed and their hooves skidded as they drew to a chaotic halt. From beneath, he heard groans and curses from the guard and Markham. And from further behind came screams of human and equine fright. For the first time, Richard became aware of another coach to their rear. This hadn't even entered his calculations. Was Catesby here then, and others? He and his lady would have to be quick then, and trust to fortune.

Richard clambered down from his seat to find Arbella waiting for him in the road. He grabbed her hand and the two of them leapt the ditch and dashed into the forest. Sounds of whinnying horses and angry voices chased them as they ran. He tugged at Arbella's hand. 'Make haste, my lady. They are close.'

After several minutes of frantic running through trees, Richard felt Arbella start to tire. 'I can't go on,' she panted, and he could hear from her wheezing breath that she was truly exhausted. He had wanted to run much deeper into the forest. If they had to stop here, they would have to find a good place to hide. He pulled her into a leafy copse next to a clearing, and they fell into a crouch.

Within a minute they heard shouts and hoofbeats approaching. Peering through the undergrowth, Richard glimpsed lanterns swinging amid the trees. Two horsemen broke into the clearing. One wore the uniform of Markham's guard. The other had a tall hat and pointed beard – the unmistakeable profile of Robert Catesby. The pair galloped on by, passing within a few paces of where Richard and Arbella lay hidden. Following behind the horsemen came three men on foot: two guards and a big, strong-looking fellow in priestly vestments, with short hair that stuck up in spikes. Staggering along in their wake was Markham, a hand still clamped to his nose.

When they were all gone, Richard rose to his feet. Arbella got up too, but he whispered to her to remain where she was. He had brought with him the ropes used to bind his wrists and the sack around his neck. When knotted together, they made a decent overall length. Richard stepped out of the copse and began tying the ends of the rope to two closely spaced trees at one end of the clearing. When he was finished, the rope stretched between the trees a few inches off the ground. He tested it to make sure it was sufficiently taut, before returning to Arbella.

'Why?' she asked in a hoarse whisper.

'It's a trap,' he told her. 'They'll pass this way when they return to the coaches. If we can bring down a horseman, that's one less of them – and I can steal his weapon.'

She stared up at him, flushed of face and gleaming with perspiration, a mix of fear and excitement in her eyes. The lady had spent her life in drawing rooms being waited upon by servants. The closest she'd come to a forest was probably the orchard at her stately home. He wanted so much to protect her, yet how was he to do that? She was so fine and delicate – like a doll of porcelain and lace. What would he feed her? What would he do if she got sick? Those questions would have to be faced at some point. But first, they had to evade their pursuers.

The muffled crack of a nearby twig caused Richard to drop back into a crouch. Arbella, whose ears and reflexes were less finely attuned, was fractionally slower. 'Someone's returned,' he whispered into her ear, and he felt her tense.

Richard's eyes were better adapted than most to the gloom. Squinting, he made out a figure – one of the guards, on foot, alone, wandering back towards the clearing. The party must have split up, so they could search the area more widely. That could make things easier.

'Wait for me here,' he breathed, and he sensed, even if he could not see, her amused smile.

Why was he always saying that to her?

Keeping low to the ground, he darted silently across the clearing towards an elm tree he'd spotted earlier. It had long, spreading limbs, densely leaved – useful for gaining height and perspective, and with little risk of detection. He scrambled up its trunk and onto one of the branches. Sliding along it, he reached a position almost directly above the guard. The man was an archer. Richard gazed at his bow enviously. It was finely crafted, like the one he used to practise with at Bradenstoke before his incarceration.

He waited as the guard came within range, then dropped silently upon him. His weight, falling from ten feet, was sufficient to render the man senseless. Richard helped himself to his bow and quiver of arrows, and raced back towards the copse. He was halfway across the clearing when a searing pain ripped through his thigh. Richard staggered on a yard or two, then collapsed. With chill despair, he knew what had happened: he himself had been hit by an arrow. A second man must have been lying in wait – the guard had been the bait to draw him out. So accustomed was he to hunting dumb animals, Richard hadn't considered that his opponents might have strategies equal to or better than his own.

The pain was hot and sharp through his leg, making him dizzy. As he wriggled through the leaf litter and into the copse, the wound stabbed at his nerves ever more ferociously. 'Run!' he hissed at Arbella through gritted teeth.

She stared at him, jaw quivering, eyes brimming with tears.

He pushed her, and finally she went. Stumbling out into the open, she ran haphazardly towards the trees on the far side of the clearing.

They won't shoot her. They can't...

A man – the guard who had shot him – now broke cover and bolted towards her. Before she could reach the trees, he grabbed her and brought her savagely to the ground. Richard, in a furnace of pain, watched this and became incensed. Though lying awkwardly on his side, he managed to pull an arrow into the bow, which he laid parallel to the ground, about an inch above it. He drew back the bowstring and took aim. On a ragged out-breath, he released. The man, who was just rising to his feet, uttered an agonised bellow and keeled over. The arrow had pierced his leg just below the knee.

Arbella wriggled free of the guard's grasp and got back up.

Now fly! Richard urged her. *Fly like a bird...*

But the man's cry had alerted his fellow guard, who now came hurtling into the clearing astride his horse.

Arbella had barely recommenced her escape when he rode up to her, swooping down in his saddle, and hoisted her up behind him. It was an impressive manoeuvre, especially at such a pace. The rider whipped his horse still faster, and they raced through the clearing, back towards the road and the waiting coaches. But laying in wait for them near the ground was a rope tied between two trees…

Richard watched with both satisfaction and alarm as the horse's front legs struck the rope. He hadn't anticipated Arbella being a victim of his trap. With a screeching neigh, the horse toppled to its knees, spilling both the guard and Arbella. The guard flew headfirst into a tree and knocked himself out. Arbella fell on her back and her head hit a root. She lay very still, and for a heart-stopping moment Richard thought she might be dead. But after a few seconds she began to stir. Her hand went to her forehead, and she climbed dazedly to her feet. She began to stagger forwards.

'Not that way!' Richard shouted hoarsely after her. But she didn't hear him, and she didn't stop. He could only watch in anguish as she headed back in the direction of the coaches.

Chapter 33

Heavenly Rain

Alice sat in the coach, bound tightly by her wrists and ankles. Will was seated next to her, similarly restrained. A guard sat opposite them. The coach was stationary and driverless in the middle of the forest. A short while ago, there had been some sort of incident involving the coach in front, forcing them into a dramatic halt.

Alice couldn't imagine what had happened. Had Lady Arbella escaped? From what she'd seen of her during their brief encounter at Bradenstoke, the woman had not appeared capable of organising any such thing. A banquet maybe – these aristocratic ladies loved arranging banquets – but surely not an escape. Perhaps someone had helped her.

Whatever had occurred, it must have been serious, for Alice had observed through her coach window almost the entire party charging off into the forest: Catesby, Watson, Markham, together with three of their guards, one of whom was the coach's driver. Only one guard had been left to watch over Will and Alice, and he was a grinning fool, who liked to amuse himself by taunting Alice with his flask of water.

She was thirsty, having not been given anything to drink since the day before yesterday, and the guard knew it, for he'd been one of her jailers in the dungeon at Bradenstoke. He would hold the flask close to her lips – close enough so she could smell it. Then he'd give it a little shake, so she could hear its echoing gurgle. If she didn't react, he'd bring it even closer and shake it again. And when she couldn't bear it any longer and leaned forwards to snatch a sip, he'd jerk it quickly back, laughing. This was how he and Alice were passing the time.

Will, watching all this, was becoming increasingly incensed. Finally, with unconcealed loathing in his voice, he blurted: 'You, sir, are a toad – both ugly and venomous. Give her some water!'

'Shut-up!' smirked the guard, and he punched Will in the stomach.

Will groaned and doubled over in his seat. 'You boil, you plague-sore,' he wheezed. 'Unfit for any place but hell!'

Alice remembered Will once remarking to her

that the world could be divided into playgoers (the charming folk who came to see his plays), and bearbaiters (those who preferred to spend their free days watching animals getting tortured). This guard was definitely a bearbaiter.

Looking up at him from his bent posture, Will asked: 'What is your name, sir?'

'Why do you want to know?' sneered the guard. 'So you can slander me in one of your plays? I'm not falling for that one.' And he smacked Will hard across the jaw, leaving a red mark.

Will prodded the sore area tenderly with his tongue. 'Well, you won't mind if I call you Iago then,' he muttered.

Alice wished she was feeling stronger, and free of her bonds, so she could take this bully on. He looked quite fat and slow, and in a fair fight she was sure she'd have the better of him. But right now she was in a pitiful state, and almost all she could think about was the water sloshing about in that flask.

The flask was in his left hand, which was currently dangling out of the coach window. She wished she could stop staring at it and think about something else. But her eyes kept getting drawn back to the horn-shaped leather vessel, as her tongue tried to moisten her cracked lips.

As she stared at the flask, she suddenly saw a drop fall into its spout from above. It made a tiny splashing sound as it struck the water within. The drop was quickly followed by another, and then another.

Was it raining? she asked herself. And if so, why was it only raining into the flask and nowhere else? This was a very *singular* kind of rainfall.

She decided she had to be dreaming – her thirsty, sleep-deprived mind had conjured this fantasy. But even though she knew it couldn't be real, the reverie persisted: the drops continued to fall in increasing quantities into the flask's spout. It droppeth, she decided, as the gentle rain from heaven, into the flask beneath. But why? The guard had had his fill. Why couldn't the heavenly rain have chosen to drop into her mouth where it would really be cherished? The individual drops falling into the flask, became, briefly, an unbroken stream. Then the rain ceased. The dream was over, and Alice was left as thirsty as ever.

Sensing her desperation, the guard brought the flask back inside he coach and waved it near her lips.

'*Please!*' she begged him. 'Just one little sip…'

Laughing, he threw back his head and took a deep, gulping swig, nearly draining it.

'Ahhh!' he said luxuriantly when he'd finished, smacking his wet lips and wiping them with the back of his hand. Then he did a terrible thing. He shoved his hand back out of the coach window and upturned the flask. Alice watched in horror as the remaining water poured out onto the road.

The flask dropped from his hand, which had suddenly become strangely lifeless. Alice watched in bewilderment as his arm flopped back inside the coach. The guard's jaw, she now noticed, was slack, and his eyes had become very wide indeed, exposing the whites all around his irises. The irises then rolled up into the top of his head, and he slumped forwards, chin first, into Alice's lap. She knocked him sideways with her thigh and he toppled into a foetal position on the floor of the coach.

'What happened?' gasped Alice.

'Justice,' murmured Will. 'Sweet justice is what happened.'

They heard a sliding sound from above, and a figure dropped down from the roof of the coach. He put his head in through the window.

Alice drew an excited breath. Was this part of the dream? Or was Tom really standing there smiling at her?

Chapter 34

This Green Plot

She stared back at him in a daze as he opened the door and hauled the unconscious guard out of the coach and dumped him in the road. Then he climbed into the coach and used his knife to cut them free of their bonds.

He was real. He had to be! As was her thirst, which continued to rage like a demon.

'*Water!*' she rasped, now staring at the flask dangling from Tom's belt.

He looked up, and paled at the sight of her dry lips and the bruises on her face. 'God's teeth!' he whispered, 'what did they do to you?'

He dropped his knife, grabbed his flask and held it to her lips. She drank greedily. Nothing in her life had ever tasted so good.

When she'd drunk her fill, she flung it aside, and hugged Tom fiercely. 'Thank you!' she breathed. He seemed to tremble briefly, then relax. She closed her eyes, allowing his presence to seep into her. Sooner than she wanted, she let him go.

Will was busy pulling the last of the rope from his ankles. 'You have an agreeable habit, young man, of appearing at exactly the right moment,' he said. 'I recall you arriving at the Globe once just in time to free a jammed trapdoor bolt…'

'That was the first time we met, Mr Shakespeare,' grinned Tom.

'What did you put in the man's water?' Alice asked – for by now she'd realised Tom had been responsible for the heavenly rain.

Tom took a small leather bottle from his pocket and held it up. 'It's called ether,' he beamed. 'It sends people to sleep. Courtesy of my master, Sir Francis Bacon.'

'Excellent work!' said Will, glancing into the forest. 'However, we're not out of the woods yet. Perhaps you'd be kind enough, Tom, to jump up onto the driver's seat and remove us from this place before Sir Griffin and his friends return. I don't mind where we go, though I've heard Stratford-upon-Avon can be agreeable at this time of year.'

'What about Lady Arbella?' asked Tom. 'I was

hoping to rescue her, too.'

'If she's not in the other coach, then she's escaped,' said Alice.

'Escaped?' gasped Tom.

'Aye. Though I've no idea how she managed it.'

Just then there came a rustling sound from the trees. Someone was approaching. Tom crouched down in the coach so he couldn't be seen. He quietly drew his knife.

The foliage parted and a petite figure staggered onto the road. Alice was both relieved and delighted to see it was Arbella. Her dress was torn and dirty and her cheek was smeared with mud. With her hand pressed to the back of her head, she seemed dazed and distressed.

Alice immediately descended from the coach and ran to her. 'This way, ma'am,' she said, guiding her to the coach and helping her inside.

Tom stared in disbelief. 'Is this…?'

'Aye,' said Will. 'It's Lady Arbella. And if this were a play, I'd demand my money back, for it's all falling into place rather too conveniently for the heroes. Still, as it's not, and there are real lives at stake, including my own, I'm quite content. Moreover, there is still plenty of time for our happy ending to unravel. Would you not agree it was high time we were on our way, Tom? Did I mention Stratford is quite pleasant, and a convenient distance from here?'

'You did,' said Tom, climbing out of the coach.

But he wasn't ready to drive them away just yet, for he couldn't abandon the horse that had served him so faithfully on his two journeys to Warwickshire. For Alice and Will, there followed a tense wait while Tom unhitched one of the coach's team of horses so that Gunpowder could replace it. He fitted his horse with a collar, belly band and breeching, then ran the shafts through the loops in his saddle to secure him to the coach.

While Tom was busy with this, Will kept his eyes fixed on the forest, watching for the enemy and muttering to himself nervously. Meanwhile, Alice tried to coax Arbella to tell her story.

'How did you escape, ma'am?' she asked.

'Escape…?' muttered the lady, who seemed only fitfully aware of her surroundings. She kept touching the back of her head and wincing with pain. Alice could only assume she had fallen or been hit.

'We must go back,' Arbella suddenly whispered.

'Back?' queried Alice. 'Home, you mean. Aye, we're taking you back home.'

'Back for him…'

'For *him?*'

'He's in the forest…' murmured Arbella.

'Who's in the forest, ma'am? Did someone help you escape? Who was he? What was his name?'

'We must go back…' cried Arbella.

'We're ready!' called Tom, climbing up onto the driver's seat. He flicked his whip, and jerkily they began to move.

'Wait, Tom!' shouted Alice. 'There's someone else…'

But Tom didn't hear her, for at that moment there came an eruption of galloping hoofbeats from the forest.

Tom didn't even look behind to see who was arriving. He knew it could only be Markham and his friends. Hurriedly, he guided the horses around the coach in front, then began to drive them hard, with fierce cracks of the whip.

Alice put her head out of the window and twisted to look behind. There were three men on horseback in frenzied pursuit. She recognised the tall Catesby with his wide-brimmed hat in the lead, followed by the more portly figure of Markham, and behind him the muscular, robed silhouette of Father Watson.

Arbella was crying, pushing her hand out of the other window and grasping at the wind, until Will pulled her back inside. Alice felt bad for Arbella's rescuer, whoever he or she was, but right now their priority had to be to get the princess away.

The coach rattled and shook as Tom drove the horses at dangerous speeds around the bends of the road. Even so, when Alice peered behind again, she observed with alarm that the chasing horsemen were a lot closer. She could see Catesby's bloodless smile, and the gleam of the flintlock pistol in his fist.

'Faster!' she yelled at Tom.

'I can't!' he bawled.

Alice saw the blur of his whip flicking up and down, the blood and spittle in the corners of the horses' mouths, the whites showing in their eyes. These animals had nothing left to give.

From the rear came the steadily building crescendo of hoofbeats. Soon, the head of Catesby's horse appeared, snorting droplets of steam. The rider, her torturer-in-chief, quickly came abreast of her coach window. Half twisted in his saddle, he faced her as he rode, his dark eyes fastening onto her like sharp hooks. Then his gaze dropped to the wheels of the coach. He pointed his pistol there, and fired. There was a loud bang, and the coach shivered and lurched downwards. Catesby fired again, and then everything seemed to fall out of control.

Straight after the second bang, Alice slid sharply sideways, her hip and shoulder slamming into the coach's interior wall. From beneath came the screeching, agonized friction of a broken axle shaft dragging along the road. At the same time, she felt Will's bulk falling upon her, squeezing her ribs and knocking the breath from her lungs. There were panicked yells in the dark carriage, hysterical braying from the horses, and painful, bone-jarring bumps as the wrecked coach veered off the road and plunged into the forest. Alice tried to cling to something – anything – solid within the blurry chaos. But before she could, everything exploded in a splintering crash that ejected Alice halfway through the window, and sent poor Will careening into Lady Arbella. The yells turned to groans, as a horrid, creaking, buckling sound began. The coach tilted nauseatingly rightwards before plunging hard onto its side, leaving Alice with her face squashed against the muddy forest floor.

She felt the weight of Will and Arbella pressing down upon her, and for some moments they all lay there in the darkness in a confused jumble of legs and arms. Gradually, with muttered whimpers of pain, they began to separate themselves. As they were doing so, the door above them squeaked open, and Catesby poked his head in, alongside the muzzle of his pistol.

'Out!' he ordered them.

'Steady on, Catesby, that's our future queen in there,' said Markham's voice, a little squashed sounding, as if he was pinching his nose. Markham reached in and helped Lady Arbella out of the overturned coach. His nose was bruised and misshapen with dried blood below the nostrils.

Will managed, with much bitter complaining, to climb out by himself. Alice discovered she had fresh bruises to add to the earlier ones. Yet somehow she found the strength to follow Will out the window and then jump down to the ground.

The front corner of the coach was smashed where it had collided with a tree. The horses stood or lay on their sides neighing pitifully, until Markham walked over and cut them free of their harnesses.

Tom was lying on a patch of grass nearby. Standing over him was Father Watson with an ancient wheel-lock pistol in his hand. 'Delighted to see you again, Traitor Tom,' he snarled. 'Now you can witness the death of your beloved, closely followed by your own.'

Will glanced around the forest in puzzlement, searching for this mysterious *beloved*. Tom didn't move or react. Alice hoped he'd been stricken unconscious by his fall from the coach. She didn't want him to have to suffer any of the despair now raging through her.

Catesby lifted Lady Arbella onto his horse. She sat upright in the saddle, silent and passive, scarcely aware of what was happening. Then Catesby approached Alice, raising his pistol and taking aim at her heart. He told Markham: 'You take the princess and Shakespeare back to the other coach. Father Watson and I will deal with these two.'

Markham didn't move. 'You mean... kill them?' he asked.

'Aye... Go now, if you don't want to look.'

'In c-cold blood?'

'It's the only kind of blood, my friend, if you wish to do this work.'

'God's work,' muttered Watson, studying Tom as he prepared to kill him.

A dark curtain was descending over Alice's mind. So this was to be the final scene for her and Tom, here in this moonlit forest glade. There would be no last minute escape. The bullet would come for her, before she could move an inch.

'This is madness,' said Will. 'I won't write another word if you do this.'

'You will, sir,' said Catesby, 'or the next thing to spark in that great mind of yours won't be an idea but a bullet.'

Alice glanced once more at Tom where he lay upon the ground. The scene was oddly beautiful. Moonlight fell upon the grass around him like pale satin. There were worse places to die – worse places for their final performance. 'This green plot shall be our stage,' she whispered – words she remembered from *A Midsummer Night's Dream*.

'Make it quick then, for God's sake,' Markham said to Catesby. 'Don't stretch it out so.'

Finally, Alice's thoughts turned to her brother Richard. She would see him again very soon, and they could go riding together in the forests of Heaven.

'Close your eyes,' Catesby said, and Alice wasn't sure if he was talking to her or Markham. She decided to keep hers open, watching his finger begin to squeeze down on the trigger, for she was determined to look death in the face as it flew towards her.

Chapter 35

A Stranger's Likeness

Robert Catesby never managed to pull the trigger. Something whispered in the night and then he started screaming and the pistol fell to the ground unfired. As he collapsed, Alice saw an arrow had pierced his right arm, just above the wrist. His blood was spattering the grass and leaves.

Immediately after that, she heard a low whistle and a thud, followed by a deep animal howl from Father Watson. Turning to look, she observed him tearing an arrow out of his dripping red hand. His firearm, too, had fallen to the ground.

Seeing all this, Markham prostrated himself in absolute terror.

Alice inhaled deeply, filling her lungs with air she'd never expected to breathe again. Her brain was struggling to process anything at this moment beyond joy, gratitude and relief.

She and Tom were alive! Someone had saved them!

Catesby, meanwhile, was crouching like a trapped hare, eyes fearfully darting about in search of their attacker. He tried to pick up the flintlock with his left hand, but was shaking so much he dropped it.

Watson, clutching his own shattered hand, uttered a defiant bellow and charged at a clump of trees at the edge of the glade from where the arrows had emanated. Before he could get there, a young man stepped out from behind one of the trees, his bowstring taut, arrow drawn against Watson's chest.

'Not a step further, old man, or this one will stop your heart,' he said.

Watson stumbled to a surly halt.

The young man was leaning against the trunk of one of the trees, and he spoke with a slight gasp, as if in pain. He was mostly in shadow, and very hard to see. Alice assumed he was the mystery person who had earlier tried to rescue Arbella. The timing of his return had been perfect, and she wanted to shout her thanks. Yet something held her back. This was not through lack of gratitude. There was just something about the young man – his voice, his stance. He reminded her very much of Richard. Of course he couldn't be, but the resemblance made her uncomfortable. Her brother was a unique and treasured part of her, now enshrined in memory. How could anyone alive dare to resemble him?

'Prithee, tie them up,' the archer said, keeping his eyes fixed on Watson. Alice sensed he was addressing her. She went to the overturned coach and clambered up the axle shaft, then reached in through the open door for some of the rope they'd earlier discarded.

'That one first,' said the young man, nodding at Watson.

'Protestant scum!' the priest growled at her as she started tying him to a tree. He kicked at her, and she had to back away.

'Do that again and you'll have an arrow in your foot to match the one in your hand,' said the young stranger.

It was disturbing how much like Richard he sounded.

As she finished tying up Watson, there was a sudden crackling of leaves behind her. She spun around, expecting an attack from Catesby. Instead she observed him flying off in the other direction, staggering deeper into the forest.

'He'll die out there,' remarked Alice.

'A lingering death, one hopes,' said Will. 'With forest worms feasting on the festering meat of his arm.'

Markham smiled at this. He was no longer prostrate, but sitting up, legs crossed, looking almost cheerful. 'Catesby is a survivor,' he said. 'I dare say, he'll live to fight another day… Unlike me.' He shuffled backwards on his bottom until he had his back against a tree. 'Tie me up,' he told her.

While she bound him to the tree, Will offered water to Tom, who was just starting to wake up.

'Where am I?' he murmured.

'In a better place than you were a while ago when we crashed,' replied Will. 'We all are.'

Alice ran to Tom and helped him to his feet, hugging him.

'I thought we were going to die,' he said.

'You have no idea how close we came,' she replied. 'But someone saved us.'

'Who?'

She turned to indicate their saviour, who now limped out of the shadows into the moonlight.

When she saw him, Alice felt the earth turn to mist beneath her. She was floating. No, she was falling – her legs no longer able give support. Tom ran to her, raised her back to her feet. But she couldn't take her eyes off the archer. Was this Heaven then? Had Catesby really shot her just now and she hadn't noticed? No, it couldn't be. Watson and Markham were still here, and they had no place in her Heaven. Yet what else could explain the appearance of her brother?

She tried to steady herself, and regain control of her breathing. It couldn't be Richard. He'd been dead these past two and a half years, drowned in the Thames. And yet, if it wasn't him, could he ever have a more perfect double?

It was true, she'd never found his body, but she'd found his treasured locket, the one belonging to their mother, on the river's muddy beach. And she'd read the coded message instructing the assassin to kill him. More importantly, he hadn't returned. If by some miracle he'd survived, he would surely have come back to the Globe, or at least sent word to her.

No, this couldn't be Richard. And if she needed any more proof of this, it lay in his expression, for when he looked at her it was with the eyes of a stranger.

Will, similarly beguiled by the stranger's familiar appearance, started towards him. 'Richard…? Richard Fletcher? Is that you?'

'Aye,' smiled the archer. 'You have my name right. Then do I know you, sir?'

'Of course you do!' laughed the playwright. 'I'm Will Shakespeare. But this is extraordinary.' He turned to Alice. 'Adam, it's your brother!'

Alice couldn't speak. Too many emotions. He had the same name! And when he smiled just now… No two people in the world could smile like that. With every passing moment in his presence, the doubts eroded and the impossible became increasingly real.

'Adam?' said Will, concern in his voice.

Her mouth was opening and closing, struggling for words and breath. There were hot tears on her cheeks. Here was her *brother!* Yet why didn't he know her? What had happened? Was this why he'd never come back?

She stumbled across the glade and threw her arms

around him, letting her head sink against his warm chest. As she did so, all the aches from her beatings faded and she felt a sense of peace that was deeper than any she could recall.

'I would not have dared to write such an ending,' she heard Will murmur.

'Are you my brother, or my sister?' Richard asked eventually.

She looked up at him, frowning. There was an odd blankness in his eyes. 'Don't you know me, Richard?'

'I've dreamed of you,' he said. 'But in my dreams, you were a girl.'

'Dreamed of me?' She shook her head in confusion. 'What happened to you?'

'It's a long story. I'll tell you about it some time. And I want to hear your story, too. But before all that, we have to get away from here.'

He turned to Arbella. 'My lady,' he said.

Arbella blinked, emerging from her daze, then smiled at him. 'Richard! I'm so glad you made it.'

'And I you, my lady,' replied Richard.

Alice flicked a glance between them, and smiled. She could see a friendship, and perhaps something more, had formed there.

Richard tried putting weight on his injured leg, and winced. 'Prithee, help me, Adam, if you would, back to the coach.'

'You're hurt!' cried Alice, staring at the wound in his leg.

'It's nothing,' said Richard, but he leaned on her gratefully, and they began to walk.

Will followed them, leading Catesby's horse with Lady Arbella in the saddle. Bringing up the rear came Tom, riding Gunpowder.

'And what about me?' asked Markham. 'You'll take me with you, won't you?'

'Judas!' Watson snarled at him.

'Don't leave me with the priest!' pleaded Markham. 'He'll eat me alive.'

'You chose to keep such company,' said Tom as he trotted away.

'I have secrets!' Markham cried after him, struggling against his ropes. 'I'll tell you anything you want to know!'

Tom halted his horse. Perhaps Markham would be useful to them after all.

He returned and untied him from his tree, then used the same rope to bind Markham's wrists, attaching the other end to the back of his saddle. As he was doing this, Watson kept up a steady stream of abuse directed at Markham. 'Viper!' he shrieked. 'Back-stabber! Turncoat! Renegade! Scab!'

Back on his mount, Tom returned to the road, with Markham stumbling along in his wake.

All the while, Watson's curses rang out through the forest: 'Bootlicker! Maggot! Apostate! Devil-spawn! You'll burn in Hell for this!'

Epilogue

LONDON, 16 TH MAY 1603

Tom and Alice sat in a pair of tall, uncomfortable chairs in Lord Cecil's gloomy office in Whitehall Palace. Cecil showed little emotion as he spoke to them, he simply stated the facts: 'Sir Griffin Markham and Father William Watson are in the Tower on charges of high treason. As for Catesby, he's vanished, and none of my contacts have any idea where he might be.'

The room was cold, despite the warm sunshine outside. It was always cold in this room, Tom imagined, like the blood running through the Beagle's veins. Tom had pleaded for Cecil to show mercy to Markham, who was the least evil of the three conspirators, and the only repentant one. But Cecil placed all 'papists' in the same basket – the one marked *traitor*. The only ones he was prepared to save from the hangman's noose were those who could be useful to him – those with information. Markham had plenty of information, and had been only too willing to share it. Sadly for him, the information he had turned out to have little value.

'I want to thank you both for all the work you've done,' continued Cecil. 'It was a close-run thing. The plotters had planned to murder the king shortly after his arrival in London at the end of May, and replace him with Arbella. And they very nearly slipped the net by feeding us with false information about decamping to Northumberland. How fortunate, Tom, that you decided instead to follow your instincts and return to Bradenstoke.'

Tom felt the press of the incriminating scroll against his leg. He'd rescued it from Sir Francis's office on his return to York House that morning and it was now safely in his pocket. If he'd returned to London just one day later, the letter would have been opened and his treason exposed. As soon as he had the chance, he would destroy it. That way, no one would ever know – although some, such as Cecil, might *suspect*... He was looking very intensely at Tom, the faintest and most cynical of smiles playing upon his lips. This man could see deep into the hearts of others, and he always seemed to find the darkness and the lies.

'Having good instincts is part of the armoury of a spy,' said Cecil, still with that cynical smile. 'Loyalty and honesty to your superiors are other vital qualities...' He let the remark hang in the air for a moment like a noose. Then he turned to Alice. 'Another quality is bravery. Adam, your nocturnal break-in to Bradenstoke was a feat of exceptional courage as well as skill. You should be proud of yourself. I know you suffered torture under Catesby, and I know you gave away nothing. Your reticence in speaking of this does you great credit. In short, you have both served your country well.

'However, the danger is far from over. Catesby, we must assume, is still at large, and no doubt there are new plots being hatched as we speak. I hope I can count on you both to heed your country's call when it next arises, as it most certainly will, and do your duty.'

After they left Cecil's office, Tom asked Alice: 'How did you do it? How did you not crack under the torture while you were at Bradenstoke?'

Alice thought about this. 'I went deep inside myself,' she replied after a moment. 'Maybe it's my training as a player. I tried to become a different person. They never reached the real me.'

'Few people have managed that,' Tom murmured under his breath.

'What did you say?'

'Nothing.'

They walked side by side in silence down the long corridor of Whitehall Palace. Tom was thinking about what a good and brave spy Alice had turned out to be, and how he wasn't at all sure he could acquit himself so well if he was ever in a similar situation.

They exited through a set of iron-studded oak doors into a vast courtyard.

Alice said: 'I suppose this is what we are now. Whether we like it or not, we're spies, working for Lord Cecil. We have to live with secrets, and tell lies, for England...'

'You've had some practice at that,' remarked Tom. 'By which I mean, you've had to live with a secret, have you not, *Adam?*'

She glanced at him: 'As have you, Tom, or so I learned from Father Watson while I was at Bradenstoke.'

This took Tom by surprise. 'What did you learn?' he asked.

'That you are...' She hesitated. 'That you are enamoured of me, Tom.'

Tom blushed. 'It was a misunderstanding,' he said hastily, using a finger to tug his ruff clear of his neck, which was suddenly feeling rather hot. 'George the wine boy saw us behind the Anchor Tavern that day, when we kissed each other farewell. He interpreted the kiss as a sign of love, and reported this to Watson.'

'Just a misunderstanding then,' said Alice in a somewhat flat tone.

'Aye. So you can rest easy, my friend.'

For the rest of their journey through the palace grounds, Alice did not speak again, or smile. The guards parted as they passed beneath the portcullised gatehouse and emerged onto the concourse at the front of the palace, where Richard and Sir Francis were waiting for them. Richard had a walking stick.

Alice's smile returned when she saw her brother. She ran to him. 'Richard, what do you think?'

'It's beautiful,' he said, gazing in wonder at the palace.

'My barge awaits,' said Sir Francis, ushering them down the balustraded stone steps that led to the river. Alice took her brother's arm and helped him negotiate the steps.

'Tom and I will be returning to York House,' said Sir Francis. 'Now that England is safe again, at least for the moment, we can return to other tasks. This afternoon, I wish to look into the possibilities of using boiling hot steam as a kind of power to propel machines. Would you care to help me, Tom?'

'Is it safe, sir?'

'Safe?' cried Sir Francis. 'Of course it isn't safe! But it will be enormous fun.'

'In that case, I would love to.'

Sir Francis and Tom disembarked at York House, and Sir Francis instructed the oarsmen to take Alice and Richard on to Southwark. Half an hour later, the two of them arrived in front of the Globe.

Richard gazed up at the white, half-timbered walls of the playhouse.

'Do you remember it?' Alice asked him.

He shook his head. 'Not really.'

She linked her arm in his. 'Come on! Let's go in. Gus Phillips and the others will be overjoyed to see you again. And when you see them – when you see the stage – it may all start coming back to you.'

'Will Mr Shakespeare be there?'

'I fear not,' said Alice. 'He is busy on his new play, *Othello*.'

She began to guide him towards the entrance, but Richard hesitated.

'Prithee, give me a moment,' he said. 'Everything is still a little... overwhelming. Just a few weeks ago I was convinced the whole world was forest. In some ways, I miss all that – the quietness, and the low green light coming through the trees.'

'You always did love the countryside, even when you were living here in Southwark,' said Alice. 'You used to escape there as often as you could, with your bow and arrow. Sometimes you took me.'

'I think I dreamed of those times when I was a prisoner at Bradenstoke,' nodded Richard. 'Only in the dreams, you were always a girl.'

Alice bit her lip. 'It's time I told you my secret,' she said. 'I couldn't say anything before, on the journey, because Will was there, and he doesn't know – at least I don't think he does...'

'Doesn't know what?'

'I'm not your brother, Richard.'

'You're not?' He looked disappointed.

'I'm your sister. My name is Alice.'

Frowning, he studied her from head to toe.

'Don't be so surprised,' pouted Alice. 'Do I look that much like a boy?'

He shook his head. 'Not now that I've looked at you more carefully, Alice.' And he uttered a joyful laugh. 'God-a-mercy! A sister! I have a sister! Why did I not see it before? You look…'

'Every inch a girl,' Alice finished. 'That's what Tom always says. He, um… He also knows the truth about me.'

'And he likes you?' Richard asked.

'Yes, we like each other.'

'Will you marry him?'

'Oh no, we're just friends.' When she saw his perplexed look, she added: 'It's easy for me to be friends with a boy when society thinks I'm a boy, too. Nobody raises their eyebrows when we're together.'

'I suspect it's more than friendship between you,' said Richard. 'You love each other, don't you?'

'Tush, what nonsense,' declared Alice, blushing a little. Then she decided to turn the same weapon upon Richard. 'But what about you and Lady Arbella? I saw the looks passing between you on the journey.'

'Lady Arbella has gone back home,' said Richard a little sadly. 'She will marry the man she loves, and forget all about me, which is how it should be, for we inhabit different worlds. She is the cousin of the king, and I am a nobody…'

'A nobody who saved her life. She will never forget

you, Richard. I can promise you that.'

He offered a tight-lipped smile, but did not reply.

'Are you ready yet, Richard?' Alice asked.

'Ready for what?'

'For this,' she said, gently leading him towards the entrance of the Globe. 'It's time you reacquainted yourself with *your* world.'

Richard swallowed. 'Aye,' he replied. 'I suppose you're right.' He paused when he spotted the Latin inscription above the entrance.

'*All the world's a stage,*' Alice translated.

'Not all of it,' said Richard. 'Some of it is forest. But that part's behind me now.'

He took a firmer grip on her arm, and together they walked into the playhouse.

Sneak preview of

The Shakespeare Plot

Book 3

The

Powder Treason

Chapter 1

The Warehouse

PORT OF LONDON, 30ᵗʰ OCTOBER 1605

Tom Cavendish crouched in the shadows behind a pillar in the old warehouse, watching. A few yards away, near the warehouse entrance, two men were heaving barrels onto the back of a waiting cart. Tom had to be extremely quiet and still. It was vital that neither of the men knew they were being observed. One of the men was small and thin, and struggled to lift his end of each barrel. The other was taller but just as slender, and Tom immediately identified him as the more dangerous of the two. He couldn't see him very well in the poor light, but what he did see made him nervous – something to do with the man's wiry build, gaunt face and long yellow teeth.

The double doors of the warehouse stood wide open, admitting a block of dusty sunlight, together with the usual sounds of the quayside – the creak of ships, the shouts of dockers and the grind of the treadwheel cranes. The Port of London, on the north bank of the Thames, was England's gateway to the world. The produce of faraway kingdoms and empires, after weeks on the high seas, all fetched up here in this warehouse and others along the bank. Inside these crates and barrels was glassware from Venice, olive oil and dried fruit from Spain, furs from Russia, tobacco from the West Indies, cotton from Africa, silk from Persia, porcelain from China and spices from the East Indies. He could smell the sweet, woody aroma of nutmeg. Tom recognised it because his master, Sir Francis Bacon, insisted on using this luxury spice to season his pastries.

Right now, the thought of serving up a nutmeg-seasoned pastry to Sir Francis in his library was very comforting. He would prefer to be doing that than squatting here in the cold shadows, squashed uncomfortably between a pillar and a coil of heavy iron chains stacked against the wall.

Sometimes, after Tom had served Sir Francis his snack, he would invite Tom to tarry a while and talk, unless he was very busy (Tom was never too busy to decline an invitation to tarry in Sir Francis's company).

His master would go to one of the shelves of his vast library and take down a volume by someone like Thomas Aquinas or William of Ockham, and he would read out a passage. Then he would pose a question arising from this, which Tom would try to answer as best he could, and this would result in a conversation, which could last for an hour or more.

It was unusual for a serving boy to be treated by his master like this, almost as an equal, but then Tom was not typical. From the moment they met, Sir Francis had recognised in Tom someone who shared his curiosity about the world. He also knew that he would never have complete authority over him in the way that masters traditionally had over their servants. He had to share him with another far more powerful person. Namely, the king. For Tom had another job – a very secret job. When he wasn't working in the service of Sir Francis Bacon, he was working as a spy in the service of England. And this was how he came to be crouching here in a cold, dusty warehouse watching two unsavoury characters heaving barrels onto a cart.

That morning, Tom had been summoned to Whitehall Palace to see Lord Robert Cecil, the king's spymaster. Cecil made these summonses from time to time. It was always unexpected, always urgent, and Tom was obliged to drop everything and come at once, no matter what he was doing. Sir Francis never complained. In his words, 'My needs can wait, Tom. The king's cannot.'

When Tom arrived there, Cecil explained the situation. A shipment of French wine had arrived at the Port of London the previous evening. There was nothing unusual about that, of course. French wine was arriving in London all the time. But an eagle-eyed customs official had noticed an irregularity in the paperwork, which he'd brought to Cecil's attention. This led Cecil to suspect that the wine in the barrels might be illegal. In other words, the exporters had not paid the customs duties payable by all those who wished to trade with England.

Most administrators, when faced with a case like this, would simply move in and arrest the smugglers and force them to pay what was owed, plus a hefty fine – but not Cecil. For Cecil reckoned there might be something deeper and darker going on. This illegal wine, so his theory went, had been brought here to be sold to raise money for nefarious purposes. When Cecil said nefarious purposes, what he really meant was 'a papist plot'. In other words, a Catholic plot to overthrow the king of England.

This would be quite an extraordinary leap of logic for most people, though not for Cecil. For he was the sort of person who saw Catholic plots everywhere. As a result, he had no difficulty in linking a cargo of dodgy wine with a conspiracy to topple the king. His fellow courtiers laughed at him. They called him the Beagle on account of his small size, but also because he was so dogged in his obsessions. The Beagle, so they claimed, would suspect a migrating bird of papist sympathies if that bird happened to winter in Catholic Spain. Yet even his sternest critics had to admit that for more than ten years, the Beagle had kept England safe.

'Discover the customer, Tom,' Cecil had instructed his young spy. 'Find out where the barrels are going. That way we'll be able to trace the link between the wine and the conspiracy.'

'There almost certainly isn't a conspiracy,' Tom had wanted to say. But he'd held his tongue because he feared and respected the Beagle far too much to argue with him. And now, several hours later, here he was, watching these men (who were almost certainly small-time smugglers and not papist plotters or anything of that sort) load the barrels onto the cart and wondering how the devil he was supposed to find out where they were going.

By now the eight large barrels had been loaded, and the cart was visibly sagging under their combined weight. The smaller of the men was busy tying a rope across the rear of the cart to secure the barrels in place. 'Where shall I take them, Mr Keyes?' he asked.

Keyes replied: 'Take them to Mr Roberts on Lower Marsh in Lambeth, go straight there, mind, no stopping for an ale at the tavern, for you'll need all your wits about you to navigate the roads down Lambeth way, them being highly treacherous, partikerly in the dark and the fog, and there's always fog in Lambeth, one slip and you're in the marsh, not that me or Mr Roberts will shed too many tears about that, as it's the safety of the barrels what concerns us, you is expendable Mr Wright, but the barrels, they is not, they have to reach Mr Roberts in perfick condition, otherwise, even assuming you survive the marsh, you is not leaving Lambeth except in a coffin.'

Keyes spoke these words in a continuous stream without once drawing breath, and all the while keeping his eyes fixed like shiny grey pins on Mr Wright.

After listening to this speech, Tom thought: I do not want to cross paths with this man. No way. And no sooner had this thought flashed through his brain, than disaster struck…

Over the past few minutes, Tom's left leg had started cramping, and in an effort to get the blood flowing through it again, he shifted position. This caused the coil of chains he was leaning against to make an audible clinking sound. The two men immediately turned their heads in his direction. Tom froze.

'Is someone here, Mr Keyes?' murmured Wright.

Keyes didn't reply. He drew his sword and began clambering over sacks and boxes towards where Tom was hidden. Tom squeezed himself more tightly behind the pillar, trying to make himself as small as possible, keeping his head down in case Keyes glimpsed the whites of his eyes. He could hear the man blundering about in the darkness, kicking over urns and poking his sword into hessian sacks.

'Probably just a cat or a rat,' suggested Wright.

Keyes stopped moving then, and Tom prayed he'd given up – until he felt something sharp and cold pressing into the back of his neck: the tip of a sword.

'On yer feet, sonny boy,' growled Keyes.

Grimacing, Tom got up, keeping his back to the smuggler.

'Who are you?' Keyes demanded.

'No one.'

The sword tip nudged forwards, biting into Tom's skin.

'Answer me!' the man snarled.

'I'm a docker.'

'And why would a docker be sitting back here in the shadows spying on us?'

'I wasn't spying on you. I was… having a rest.'

Tom was taking advantage of the darkness to slowly draw his sword.

'I say you was spying on us.'

'You're wrong.'

'Who sent you?'

Tom suddenly whirled around and batted Keyes' sword away with his own. He'd hoped to smash it from his hand, but Keyes maintained his grip on the weapon. Desperate to maintain the advantage of surprise, Tom barged into the taller man's chest, causing him to stumble backwards. But before he could bring his sword to Keyes' throat, the smuggler slithered away, deeper into the shadows.

Tom peered around, trying to gauge where the man had got to. Then he heard the swish of Keyes' sword,

followed by the crack of splintering wood and an
ominous rumble. Acting on pure instinct, Tom dived
to his left just as half a dozen heavy barrels rolled off
a collapsing shelf and crashed to the floor where he'd
been standing. Keyes had meant to crush him.

While Tom was still on his knees, a line of gleaming
steel flashed out of the darkness towards his head. At
the last second, he raised his sword and parried Keyes'
blade. He could see the man's yellow-toothed leer as he
tried to keep Tom pinned to the floor. Keyes pressed
mercilessly downwards, crushing Tom's sword hilt
against his chin. Tom rammed his knee into the man's
ankle. Keyes staggered from this unexpected assault,
and Tom was able to squirm out from beneath him and
regain his feet. He leapt onto a box and aimed a sudden
blow at Keyes' neck. Sparks flew as Keyes parried and
then pushed back. Tom came at him again. Savagely
they attacked each other, smashing sword against
sword with all their strength, searching for a weak
point in the other's defence.

Tom had a height advantage, thanks to the box.
He'd also been trained well, first by Sir John Davies
at Essex House, and more recently by Robert Armin
of the King's Men, who was giving him weekly lessons
paid for by Lord Cecil. He knew the importance of
posture, balance and lightness of feet. He knew how
to keep his blade close and his movements firm yet
controlled so as not to expose himself to counter-
attacks. His disciplined style seemed to anger his

adversary who was becoming increasingly wild in his swings and thrusts. Tom stayed calm, waiting for his opportunity. When Keyes was late to a block, Tom's sword tip sliced close to the man's neck, severing his leather necklace. A thin line of blood appeared near his throat. Keyes hissed with rage and flew at him. Tom side-stepped and brought his sword down in a classic counter-stroke that would have lopped off his opponent's arm.

Would have.

A second before his sword could meet its target, Tom was shoved violently in the back. He toppled off the box, landing in a painful heap on the floor. Before he could get up again, Keyes thrust his sword towards his chest. Tom looked up into the man's murderous red eyes. Cowering in Keyes' shadow was his smaller companion, Wright. It must have been he who had crept up behind Tom and pushed him over.

Keyes laughed throatily, exposing his evil, wolf-like teeth. 'Any last words, spy, before I end your miserable existence?'

TO BE CONTINUED...